Ashes Beneath the Altar

Kaiden Hanks

Ashes Beneath the Altar

Paperback: 979-8-9954742-0-3
E-book: 979-8-9954742-1-0

Cover art and interior design by Heidi Sutherlin

Printed in the United States of America.

Eldredge Press

Chapter One

I don't believe in signs. Or fate. Or divine warnings blinking at me through half-dead lightbulbs. But if I did, the flickering above my bathroom mirror might mean something. It's been doing that for weeks—buzzing like it's caught between giving up and holding on. And honestly, most days, I can relate.

I brush my teeth in the same rhythm like I always do. I rinse, swish around my mouthwash and meet my tired eyes in the mirror. I haven't slept in days. My dreams won't let me. Most of the time, I don't remember them—but I can remember smoke and something burning.

I flick off the bathroom light and trudge into the kitchen to make some coffee. The coffee maker rattles and the house groans as if it resents being awake this early. Fair enough. I pour my coffee, ignore the pile of mail, and shrug on my jacket. It's colder than it should be for October. Fog clings to the windows like its begging to be let in from the cold. I hate to tell it, but it's not much warmer in here. I drink my coffee as quickly as I can and set the mug in the empty sink. One of the perks of living alone is only having yourself to clean up after.

I grabbed my backpack off the table and slipped on my Nikes. I plucked my keys off the hook by the door and locked it from behind me. Tossing my bag into the backseat, I cranked my car and turned the heat up as high as it could go. I let out a deep breath, threw on my seatbelt, and pulled out of the driveway.

My job is a pretty quiet one. I am the Special Collections Assistant at the county library, which is really just a fancy way of saying that I spend my days in a basement with books no one checks out and documents no one remembers. If I'm being honest, I wouldn't have it any other way. The library is only 15 minutes from my house, so the drive is over almost as soon as it begins. I parked in my usual spot and grabbed all my things. I'm usually the first one here for the first hour, then my coworkers start coming in. I unlocked the familiar door and locked it again once I'm inside the building.

The library has always smelled of dust, paper, and, oddly enough, pipe smoke, even though no one has been allowed to smoke in here in decades. The morning light filters through the tall windows. This place was beautiful once, with brightly colored stained glass and carved wood details that people don't notice or appreciate anymore. Now, it's just a quiet building that holds memories.

Half the lights don't work, and we are down to a skeleton staff. I make my way to the flight of stairs leading to my office in the basement. My placard reads "Special Collections." To most that would sound important, but really, it means I spend most of my day alone, cataloging forgotten books and brittle newspapers from the 1800s—lost echoes of a time that feels distant, even to me.

As I reach my office, I flick on the old lamp above my desk. Its warm glow reveals a stack of folders I'd left half-finished yesterday, a chipped mug of pens, and a leather-bound book that hadn't been there before. I tilt my head at it as if it can see my confusion. Setting my bag down in the chair, I search for a note from my boss about the books purpose. Its brown leather, cracked and curling up at the corners. A faint symbol burned into the spine—circular, almost resembling an eye. I reached out, running my fingers over the cover. What lies within?

I am startled when I hear the floor creak overhead. Exhaling, I tell myself it's probably just Miriam, here early, and wrestling with the old coffee machine in the break room. I make a mental note to ask her about the strange leather-bound book later and I set it aside. Settling in my creaky chair, I opened a folder I had left from yesterday.

I was halfway through labeling a set of handwritten letters when Miriam's voice floated down the stairwell. "You down there, Piper? Or did the ghosts finally get you?" I chuckle, "I'm here," I called back, not looking up. My voice echoes more than I expected. Her footsteps thud down the stairs, and a moment later, she pops her head around the door frame, holding two steaming paper cups like peace offerings. Miriam was one of those people who made too much eye contact and smiled all the time, which throws me off balance.

She hands me one of the cups. "Hazelnut. I know you usually go for black coffee, but I thought I'd risk it." I took it from her and offered a smile. "Thank you, Miriam." She leans against the door frame, her grin widening. "See, you do have a smile." I gave her a look, but she just grinned and moved to lean against the filing cabinet across from me. She was dressed in her usual cardigan- over- floral-dress combo, her hair twisted into a messy bun, and glasses perched on her nose. "Did you sleep last night?" less teasing now, her voice softens. "You look..."

"Like I've been resurrected from the dead?"

"I was going to say, 'like you didn't sleep', but sure, we'll go with that." She takes a sip from her coffee, eyeing me. "I'm fine," I lied, taking a sip of coffee, so she'll stop looking at me like I'm about to fall apart. Miriam's gaze flicked to the leather-bound book on my desk. "That new?" I shrug, "I'm not sure, but I don't think so. I haven't logged it yet. No one left me a note or call number for it."

She stepped closer, squinting at it. "Weird. Kinda looks.... old. Like *old*-old." I nodded in agreement, and we both sat in an unsure silence. After a moment, she turned to me and said, "If it starts whispering Latin to you, I'm leaving and never coming back." I forced a laugh. "Fair enough. I'll be right behind you." She lingered another second like she wanted to say more, then pushed off the filing cabinet. "I'll be upstairs if you need me. Try not to summon anything strange." I propped my chin my palm, "Noted. I don't believe in that stuff anyways."

When she was gone, I looked back at the book. It looked eerie, so I tucked it into my top drawer until Velicity arrives hoping that she could shed some light on it. I stayed working on the letters for a while. Handwritten in ink so faded it was almost impossible to decipher. Civil War correspondence, I think— love and longing penned in cursive loops that no one uses anymore. I catalogued, labeled, and sealed each one into its acid- free folder. It was mechanical work, but I liked it.

Around ten, the overhead lights flickered once. It frightened me and I shook my head at myself. In this old building, things like that happened all the time. But then the bulb over the desk began to buzz. It was a long, low hum that didn't match the usual fluorescent flicker. Goosebumps peppered my skin. I didn't like this feeling, so I reached over and turned the light off. I headed upstairs to get a break from the room.

After lunch (if you can call cold coffee and a granola bar lunch), I made my way to the main part of the library to reshelve some books that someone had left in the theology section. On my way back to my office, I noticed dust coating everything. It's weird these are out: No one has checked out a Bible commentary in several years.

I reached for a copy of Angels in the Old Testament, its spine worn and torn. As I went to put it back where it belonged, I froze. The same symbol that had been on the strange leather book downstairs, is faintly imprinted on the edge of the shelf— almost invisible unless the light hits it just right. I rubbed it with my thumb, staring at it in confusion. I shrugged my shoulders, then walked away without shelving the rest of the books.

Back in my office, Miriam pops her head in just before closing. "Are you okay?" she asked, brows furrowed. "Yeah, I'm just tired." She gives me a look that indicates she doesn't believe me. "You sure? You look like one of those exhausted cartoon ghosts I've seen on TV." I force a chuckle, "Well, I guess I work in the right place to be affiliated with ghosts." She snorts. "Can you lock up for me? Velicity never showed up today. Maybe I got her vacation days wrong, and she returns tomorrow." I nod in agreement. Miriam is a nice person but she's a talker and I am most definitely not. "Yeah, no problem. I got it." She leaves with a smile and a wave. I watched the stairwell until her footsteps faded.

I shut the library down like I always did: turning off lights, checking locks, and unplugged the coffee pot. I have an irrational fear of fires and read that plugged in appliances can cause fires even when they're not in use, so I just make it a point to unplug them. Plus, it's always a little amusing to watch someone get frustrated because the coffee pot isn't working. I went back downstairs to grab my bag and lock up my office, but when I opened my drawer to get my keys, I quickly noticed that the book was gone. Odd. I know I didn't move it, and Miriam doesn't come in here unless she's poking at my emotions. I began searching for it, thinking I might be going crazy and had moved it. I didn't see it anywhere.

I'll be the first to admit that the shadows in the corners of the room, seem heavier than usual. This is one of those times when I'm reading too much into something. Taking this is as a sign, I grabbed my bag and keys. As I go to turn off the light, my hand hovers just over the switch, but before I can touch it, the light flickers.

Instinctively, I turned around to face the room. My heart raced as I leaned forward and see something scrawled faintly on my desk in...pencil? I leaned forward some more to read it better.

Do you see it yet?

Chapter Two

I stared at the pencil marks for a solid ten seconds before leaning over and rubbing the words away with the sleeve of my jacket. There. All gone. But the slight uneasiness still remained in my stomach. Someone is pranking me and I'm not going to give them the satisfaction of a reaction. Or maybe it's stress, or lack of sleep. Whatever it is, I chose to ignore it.

I shoved my keys into my pocket and slung my bag over my shoulder and shut the door behind me. As I walked swiftly up the stairs, to the front door, an unsettling feeling crept over me —I felt like I was being watched. I didn't hesitate; I stepped outside and locked the door behind me.

Outside, the fog had thickened, crawling low across the pavement like ghostly fingers. I hurried to my car, unlocked it, and tossed my bag in the passenger seat. For a moment, I just sat there, taking a breath. After a few heartbeats, I turned the key. Headlights cut through the mist, illuminating the way ahead. The engine shuddered, coughed, and settled into a steady hum. I pulled out of the lot and drove home in silence, the only sound was of the gravel popping under my tires as I pulled into my driveway. This yanked me from my thoughts.

My house was cold when I walked in. I sat my bag down and kicked off my shoes and double checked the locks before making my way to the thermostat. After dialing it up a couple notches, I poured myself a bowl of cereal and sat down on my couch. I turned on the TV, even though I wasn't sure why—I rarely found anything good to watch, but I am the type of person who needed something to watch while I eat.

After I finished eating and channel surfing for what felt like forever, I finally gave up. I turned on the shower, and while it was warming up, I grabbed some flannel pajamas to change into. In an old house like this, it's best to dress in the bathroom while the warmth of the steam lingers. After my shower, I made myself a cup of tea warm tea. I've always hated tea but when I had trouble sleeping as a child, my dad would make me some, and it felt like magic. To this day, I still do it and for whatever reason, it still works. After I finish my tea, I shuffled into the bathroom to brush my teeth.

When I finally climbed into bed, I curled up into a ball, pulling the covers up to my chin. I loved my bed; it was the coziest spot in this whole house. But tonight, for some reason, that comfort eluded me. I reached up and turned off my lamp. Almost immediately, goosebumps prickled my skin. Even in the darkness, I swear I felt like I was being watched. As quickly as the feeling washed over me, so did the exhaustion from the sleepless nights. Before I knew it, I was sinking into a deep and heavy sleep.

I woke up to pitch blackness, both outside and inside my room. I blinked in the dark and a tightness settled in my chest. The numbers on my alarm clock glowed a dull red from across the room—3:17. My eyes burned, and my brain felt foggy. Something about those numbers felt familiar, and it only took a moment to remember: that was the exact time I had seen on the clock in my childhood home the day I found my dad.

I didn't move for a while; I just laid there, listening. Eventually, I sat up, pushed the blanket off, and crossed the room to the window. The glass felt cold under my fingertips. Fog pressed thick outside, giving a slightly eerie appearance. In the corner of the windowpane, I noticed a faint smudge—a gray, powdery smudge. Curiosity piqued, I rubbed it away with the sleeve of my shirt. It looked fresh, and I knew it hadn't been there the night before, because I had sat by this window reading for most of the evening.

Who knows, maybe I left it open, and the wind had carried it in from outside. But deep down I knew I hadn't. It had rained for the past 4 days so everything was too wet to burn. I stood there for what felt like an eternity, staring into the fog, almost like I was waiting for it to reveal something. But it never did, and exhaustion pulled me back to bed.

As soon as my head hit my pillow, I buried myself under the covers, telling myself I was just tired. Your mind plays tricks on you when you're tired. That's what I believed. "Science", I told myself. Sleep came swiftly, but returned with the same recurring dream; a boy standing in the middle of a burning field, looking at me and screaming my name.

Chapter Three

I enjoyed Sundays. The library was closed, giving me a full day to do whatever I pleased. Not that I just had a long list of things to do, but it was nice to have the option. Today I came to visit my dad. The cemetery looked just as it did the last time I was here. The wall surrounding it was still crumbling, perhaps even more. The iron gate creaked eerily as I pushed it open. The trees spooked me more than anything; they stood tall and skeletal, swaying in the brisk wind, almost like they're bowing under the weight of all the names buried beneath them.

I didn't come here often. My therapist suggested I make weekly visits, and always reminded me that closure isn't a door you can simply close, but a process you must walk through. I found him dead though, so coming here is incredibly tough.

The gravel crunched beneath my shoes as I made my way to the back corner of the cemetery. His headstone was simple, just like any other you'd see. I crouched beside it and set the dying flower I plucked from the side of the road on my way here.

"I still don't understand," I murmured, my voice sounding frail in the cold air. I didn't expect an answer, but I would have loved to hear his voice one more time.

Suddenly, the wind shifted, carrying the scent of something familiar and out of place—something...burnt? But how could anything be burning? I glanced around, searching for smoke, but I didn't see anything coming from either direction.

I took a deep breath and looked back down. At the base of the headstone, along the bottom edge, was a dusting of ash—thin, black as night, ash. It almost resembled soot. My stomach twisted at the sight.

I reached out and ran my finger through it; it smeared like charcoal. How did I miss that when I arrived?

I glanced over my shoulder, scanning the rows of graves, but I saw nothing—no one for that matter. The air felt heavier now. I looked back at my dad's headstone and... no freaking way... There it was—the symbol. Barely visible, carved into the stone at the bottom left-hand corner. The same mark from the book at the library and on the shelf it had been on.

A sharp feeling flickered in my chest—fear or panic; I wasn't sure which.

I wiped the ash from my fingers onto my jeans and stood up, my head spinning from standing up too fast. I turned toward the exit and started walking. I didn't say goodbye, and I definitely didn't look back.

I made a bee line for my car—or at least I tried to. Halfway there, the hairs on the back of my neck stood up. Something felt off. It felt like the very air was pressing in on me. I slowed, glancing over my shoulder.

Nothing. But the silence had changed. There were no birds or rustling trees—just the sound of my own heartbeat, pounding louder with every step. I picked up my pace, convinced I could hear footsteps behind me. I froze. *Don't turn around, Piper. Just go. Get to the car.*

My body wouldn't listen. I turned. Something was there— a shadow. Tall and hunched, wrong in every way. My mind tried to make sense of it. It didn't move, but I did. My knees buckled beneath me. I had no control over my body. My vision threatened to go black, but I fought I keep my eyes open, blinking furiously to maintain any semblance of control.

The last thing I saw was a flicker—just a brief glint of light cutting through the fog. Then everything went black.

Chapter Four

When I came to, the first thing I noticed was how comfortable I felt. I blinked my eyes open, taking in the familiar surroundings of my room. The rising sun cast a warm stream of light through my curtains. For a few seconds, I laid there, trying to piece together how I had even gotten home. The last thing I remembered was standing by my dad's grave—then nothing. Just that overwhelming feeling of being watched, then sudden dizziness, and a vague sense that the air was closing in on me.

Now, here I was—safe, but rattled to my very core. I sat up slowly, half-expecting something crazy to happen or someone to jump out and yell *boo.* But everything was calm.

Yet, it was the kind of calm that made you question whether the chaos had even happened at all, or if your mind had conjured it up.

I pushed the covers off and swung my legs over the side of the bed, wincing as my bare feet hit the cold floor. I had always preferred to keep the lights on at night because they made me feel more secure, but with the sun creeping in, I felt much safer. I made my way into the kitchen, turning off lamps, and lights on my way.

I made myself a pot of coffee and sat down at the kitchen table. I had to text Miriam and tell her I wasn't feeling well and would be taking the day off. She wouldn't push me for any other explanation, especially since I never called in, but the events of late just have me so uneasy.

Around nine, I finally dragged myself to the shower, trying to rinse the lingering feelings of dread. I hadn't realized I was shaking until I dropped the towel twice while trying to hang it up. I caught a glimpse of myself in the mirror. My dark hair was sticking up in every direction, my eyes were bloodshot, with shadows under them, so pronounced they looked sunken. For a moment, I didn't even recognize myself.

I was halfway through making toast when I saw it—sitting on the table, right where I had been sitting:

The book.

I dropped the butter knife, barely hearing it clatter against the tile. I hadn't brought it home; I hadn't even touched it, and yet there it sat, radiating an unsettling wrongness, like heat rising off asphalt.

I stood there, frozen. My thoughts raced with whirlwinds of what if's and why's.

If I read it, what would I find? Could it change everything? One thing I knew for sure; if I took that step, there would be no going back.

But if I left it there and ignored it, maybe it would disappear the same way it had appeared, taking the dreams, the ash, and the hollow whispers with it.

Yet, maybe it would linger, rotting at the center of my life until I couldn't ignore it anymore. I could vaguely smell the other piece of toast burning in the toaster, but I was frozen. The scent of it filled the kitchen, sharp and acrid, yet still, I didn't move. I couldn't move.

Because somehow, standing there in my own house with nothing but a cheap toaster and a leather book between me and whatever the heck was happening, I realized something.

It was already too late to pretend that none of this was real.

Chapter Five

I don't remember walking toward it. One second I was across the room, frozen in panic; the next, I stood at the edge of the table, the burned toast forgotten, a bitter taste already in my mouth.

The book sat like it belonged. And strangely, it felt like it's always been mine. It was starting to look familiar, but I can't place where I recognize it from.

I reached out and then hesitated, my fingers hovering over the worn leather. My heart knocked against my ribs, desperate to escape.

Don't touch it.

My father's voice- or maybe just the echo of it–I wasn't sure anymore. I took a deep breath and pressed my palm against the book.

The moment my skin made contact, the kitchen faded away.

Not literally; my feet were still on the floor, my fingers were still on the book, but something in the air definitely shifted. The light dimmed. The sound around me dropped, and even the hum of the fridge died, like someone had pulled the plug on the world.

A pressure bloomed in my chest- heavy, hot, almost ancient. It felt like I'd just opened a door I couldn't see, and heat just slapped against me.

The symbol on the spine pulsed beneath my palm, faint but alive, almost like a heartbeat. I tried to pull my hand back, but I couldn't. My fingers stayed glued to the leather as if the book wasn't done with me yet.

Then something, not really a voice, but more like a thought whispered into my mind: "You are marked."

In a surge of panic, I yanked my hand back with all my strength, stumbling against the counter hard enough to rattle the coffee pot. My chest heaved, and my palm burned. I looked down at my hand; the symbol was faintly etched into my skin. It wasn't bleeding or red like I had just been burned, it was just there, like I was born with it.

Then the lights flickered. For a single heartbeat, I wasn't alone in the kitchen. Something moved in the reflection of the window—a human shadow...with wings?

It was gone before I could blink.

Once everything became still, and the air returned to normalcy, I sank down on the kitchen floor, trying to get my bearings and get my thoughts in order.

I felt like I was going crazy.

Once my breathing returned to normal and nothing wild happened for several minutes, I stood up and moved slowly to the window, each step echoing like it didn't belong to me. I reached out, my hand trembled against the glass. The windowpane was ice cold. On the inside sill, just below where the shadow had passed, I found ash.

It was black and fine, unlike the dust I had seen before. This was thicker, almost greasy. Twisting in patterns I didn't understand. At the center were three faint finger marks.

Something had been reaching *in*.

I staggered back, shaking to my very core. The mark on my palm pulsed, like a brand that wasn't finished burning. I gripped my wrist, teeth clenched, trying to not scream. The book still sat on the table behind me, closed but humming with quiet energy, like it was alive.

I looked back at the ash, my breathing shallow.

There, just beside the greasy smear, was a small scattering of almost silver ash. It was noticeably lighter and brighter than the black ash. The air shifted again, just slightly. A chill crept up my back, but it wasn't cold. It felt protective—almost familiar in a crazy, oddly comforting way.

At this moment, I was certain of a few things: something bad was happening and I couldn't see it. Someone was looking out for me, or at least that's how it felt. And lastly, I was *marked.* I needed to figure out what that meant and what I was going to do about it because I certainly didn't want to be.

Chapter Six

Tuesday morning came in a sleepy blur.

The sky was still gray, and the air still hot and muggy. The kitchen still bore burnt toast, even though I spent most of the night trying to get the smell out. The book remained on the table, untouched; I hadn't been brave enough to handle it again.

I finished my coffee and placed the mug in the sink, then grabbed a dish towel out of the drawer. Carefully, I picked up the book, being extra careful not to touch it with my skin and wrapped it up in the towel. I shoved it into my satchel, telling myself that it's just a book and books belong in libraries, even cursed ones that leave a mark that refused to wash off.

I tried getting it off half the night to no avail. My mind waged a war over whether to google "marked one" or to embrace ignorance, hoping it will all go away. I obviously chose the latter and spent the rest of the night manic-cleaning my house, blaring music to drown my anxiety.

The library smelled the same as always. I know it sounds strange, but it brings me an odd sense of peace. I really do love this place. I took a deep breath, inhaling in the old leather, the citrus wood cleaner the janitors used, and the musty aroma of the many ancient books this building holds. I clung to this smell more than I cared to admit.

Miriam hadn't come in yet; it was just me, the buzzing of the overhead lights and the quiet groan of the heating system coming alive. I made my way down to the basement to my office, and anxiety began to creep its way back in, knowing that this is where it all started.

I carefully pull the towel-wrapped book out of my bag and set it on my desk. I almost laughed at how this book upended my life just a few hours ago. I didn't exactly know what I was expecting but I carefully unwrapped the book and then just stared at it, waiting.

If I had to guess, I'd say I sat for about 10 minutes in silence, just staring at the book. Eventually, I wrapped it back up and tucked it into my top drawer, and shifted my focus to my actual job.

I was in the zone, and before I knew it, my stomach was growled, so I decided to stop and head to the break room. Halfway up the stairs, it dawned on me that Miriam never stopped by to say good morning and I haven't heard any footsteps overhead indicating that people were here. Was I just that focused?

When I reached the break room, I didn't encounter a single person, which was strange. That had never happened before. I ate a quick salad stored in the fridge along with a protein shake. Just as I went to toss the bottle in recycling, a chill ran down my spine, and hairs all over my body stood up. I got a weird feeling in my stomach. I immediately turned around and a man stood in the doorway watching me. What the..? I didn't hear the bell of the front door ding! I didn't even hear the creak on the old hardwood floors that are impossible to be quiet on, trust me, I've tried.

He wore a gray suit, his shoes spotless and so clean they shined, with His hands folded behind his back, propped against the door frame. His eyes were dark green, and resembled the green of trees in summer.

"Hello, Piper," he said, his voice cutting through my chest like a knife. I tried to keep my panic in check, and not let him see that he had me shook.

I took a slight step back, "Do I know you?"

"No." He replied, smiling faintly. "But your father did." My breath caught in my throat. I had moved away from my hometown to escape everyone I knew, so I was a little skeptic of this man.

"I think you have the wrong person." Striving to make my voice sound strong, even though it wavered. His eyes glanced behind me then he brought them back to mine. I quickly took a glance over my shoulder, and there sitting on the table is that freaking book. You have got to be kidding me. I waited for that thing to do something, and it of course chose now.

I shot my eyes back to him trying desperately to mask my emotions. "No," he said again. "I'm exactly where I need to be." He stepped forward slowly, almost respectfully, as if I were a deer he didn't want to spook. He pulled something from his coat— it was a slip of folded paper that looked aged and crumbled. Gently, he placed it beside the book.

Then he looked at me and nodded once, "You've been marked. Don't let them in your mind." How did he know that? I felt a loss of control over my body; my breathing is quickened, and was sure my face betrayed the whirlwind of emotions I wanted to hide. There were a million things I wanted to ask, but all that came out was, "Who are you?" But he was already walking away.

"Hey!" I called out, following him through the labyrinth of hallways. "What does that mean to be marked? Who are you talking about? What do you mean 'don't let them in my mind'?" He did not answer. By the time I reached the lobby he was gone, and I was alone again.

I ran out to the parking lot and my car was the only thing there. I walked back to my office, my mind reeling, sat down at my desk and unfolded the piece of paper. It read:

Isaiah 43:2

'....When you walk through fire, you will not be burned; the flames will not set you ablaze."

Veilbreaker.

Chapter Seven

The library was empty when I left. There were no front desk staff, and Miriam and Velicity had never showed up. No one had called, texted, or even emailed me to say that they wouldn't be here or if, for whatever reason, we were closed.

I stood in the in the doorway of my office after I shut everything down, with my keys gripped tight in my hand. Call it my paranoia, but the silence just felt off. Like the building itself was holding its breath, waiting to see what would happen next. Or maybe that was just me.

As I stepped outside and locked the door to the library, I caught myself glancing over my shoulder. Once. Twice, for good measure. The air is heavy, almost thick—like something

I couldn't see was pressing in close. I felt as if was being pressed between two walls.

The street and neighborhood were normally busy with cars. Kids were typically laughing and playing while they enjoyed being home after school, and today it's eerily silent. Of course it was. I was halfway to my car when I spotted something on my windshield, I paused.

Ash.

A light smear right on my windshield. Rubbing it off with my sleeve, my heart started to beat out of my chest. The smear resembled the one from earlier— three long strokes, like the fingermarks in my kitchen. When I got into my car, I locked the doors out of instinct, and fear...mostly fear.

I did not go home right away. I drove in circles for half an hour, my knuckles hurting from gripping the steering wheel tight, and my stomach in twisted knots. When I finally pulled into my driveway, I sat in the car for a long time. I listened to the engine tick as it cooled off. The sun had almost set completely before I emerged from my car and went inside.

I dropped my bag by the door and kicked off my shoes. The book is in my bag, still wrapped up. While, in a different room, I can still feel the books presence weighing down on me.

I went straight into the kitchen, taking extra care not to look at the window or the spot at the table from earlier today. Just in case. Instead, I made a salad, grabbed a honey bun and made my way to the living room. I turned on the TV, even though I was not interested to surf the different channels. I forced myself to eat every bite of food and ignored the million thoughts racing through my mind.

However, one thought just kept coming to the surface. *You've been marked. Don't let them in your mind.*

Pushing the thought out of my head. I tried to force myself to read a book, but I could not focus and could not retain anything, so I got into the shower and got ready for bed. By the time I showered, blow dried my hair and brushed my teeth, I had myself convinced that a good night's sleep would help clear my mind, hoping to make sense of things.

I crawled into bed and got cozy under the covers. Sleep took over fast. Before I knew it, I was standing in a place that didn't resemble Earth. The ground beneath me was scorched black, pulsing with slow, red light veins beneath ash. Smoke curled at the edges of the horizon, but there was no fire. At the center of it all, half-buried in the dust, was an altar. The stone was cracked, and it was bound in rusted iron chains.

Then just beyond the altar, I was able to barely make out a shape in the smoke. It was him. The boy. He stood barefoot near the altar, white clothes streaked with ash, and his eyes sank into his face. The firelight caught something carved into his wrist. That's when I felt the entire world halt. It was the same mark that appeared on my palm.

"You're late," he said, steadily. The way he looked, he couldn't have been more than eighteen, but he sounded older. I looked around before answering him. This feels real, I can feel the heat from the ashes. "I have no clue what you're talking about or insinuating what I would be on time for." I tried not to sound sarcastic, but more so like I genuinely have no idea.

"Yes, you do," he replied with a nod. Okay, so he isn't much of a talker. Great.

"Well, what is this place?" I asked him. Looking down at his feet, he answered, "It's where everything begins." He's looking back at me now. "And where everything will burn if you make the same choices as the ones before." His voice changed to cold and serious.

"What choices?" I asked, scared to know the answer.

"The altar is sealed. The Hollow Ones want it broken. If they tear it open anymore, the Veil won't hold. Your world becomes theirs." A sharp wind cut through the heat, scattering a mix of white and black ash at our feet. "You are the last Veilbreaker," he said. "The others are gone. Killed and forgotten."

My breath caught in my throat and my heart thumped so hard it felt like it was going to jump right out of my chest. My mind raced a million miles an hour with all the questions I want to ask. When I opened my mouth to speak, the only thing that comes out was, "Why me?" I swallowed, preparing myself for the answer.

"Because your father begged. He knew you were capable of incredible things."

The air stilled and my heart sunk to the bottom of eternity. I stared at him, "What?"

He shifted on his feet, "The moment he saw you, he had an overwhelming feeling that you would save the world. After some years, he learned more about the battle we can't see, the one between angels and demons. He asked someone to protect you at all costs and to help you stop the fire no matter the cost." My heart stuttered. "Who did he ask?"

The boy turned away. "Trust me, you'll know him when you meet him." My patience was running thin with his vague answers. "What do you mean?" But he was already walking toward the altar, not noticing he had walked in front of it, while smoke swirled behind him. His voice came one last time, quiet but piercing. "They're trying to kill you, Piper. They're going to suck all that is happy and good from you. That's what they do. You will be just a shell of a person and eventually darkness will take over and you will fade into a quiet nothingness, swallowed by depression."

I jolted awake with a cry caught in my throat. My sheets were damp in sweat. I sat up and turned on the lamp beside my bed. To no surprise, there was a small pile of ash on my nightstand.

Chapter Eight

Staring at the ash, my heart pounding hard enough to shake the silence. I realized that every time I have an encounter, there is ash left behind.

The air in my room felt thick and heavy, it was getting harder to breathe. I sat up straight, and pulled my blanket around me, afraid to move. Something, or someone, had been in here, for the second time today. Not in my dream, but for real. I don't think I ever felt like I was in danger, as crazy as that sounds. But now, with the weight of everything pressing on my chest, I do not know how I can feel anything but danger.

Swallowing hard, I blink into the shadows near the closet. I wasn't sure, but I had a strong feeling, so I found the courage to ask, "If you're here to hurt me, or consume what's left of my happiness from me, whatever that means, just go ahead and get it over with." Silence. A silence so loud, I began to wonder if my gut was wrong. Then, I felt the pressure of the room change, and I could feel the presence of someone.

"If I wanted to hurt you," a deep voice said seriously, "you would've been hurt long ago." I turned sharply, blanket falling from my shoulders. He stepped forward from the far corner, where he blended into the shadows like it was his second nature.

He was tall, really tall. His face was partially obscured, like the light refused to fully reveal him. But his eyes, fixed on me with a tired certainty. It was as if he knew exactly who I was. Then the boy from my dream came across my mind and realization came flooding through.

"Who are you?" I whispered. He didn't answer right away. He just kept watching me. Then finally, he said, "I'm the one keeping the Hollow Ones off your doorstep." A beat passed. I was right in who I thought he was, and that means none of this is a dream, I confirmed that by pinching my leg and it hurt like you know what.

Then he spoke again, "And the one who promised your father I would protect you."

My mouth went dry. For a second, I didn't say anything. I couldn't. My brain was too busy short-circuiting around that last sentence. *Your Father*. He said it like it explained everything and it was supposed to make me trust him. But it didn't.

"I don't understand," I said. "My father has been dead for years. You knew him?" He didn't hesitate, "I kept my distance. But yes, I knew him. And that's all the questions I am answering tonight."

I jumped up from my bed, ignoring the ache in my chest. "Oh no, you don't get to show up in my room, drop some cryptic line about a promise you made my father, and then shut down." My voice is steadily getting louder, "If you know something, *say it.* Who on God's green Earth, are you?" He exhaled like he was bored of this conversation, which only added to my irritability. "I'm not who you're afraid of," he said. "But I'm not who you want me to be either."

LOL. He's kidding, right? "Oh good," I snapped. "You're annoying *and* vague. What a comfort." He stepped toward the window, like he was ready to leave, like he wasn't just turning my world upside down and wasn't having any empathy whatsoever. "I gave your father my word," he said quietly. "I'm here because of that. Not because of you." My heart sank. I'm not sure how much more my heart can take of this. Before I could say anything else, he paused with one hand on my curtain.

Then without turning around, he added, "You're not safe anymore, Piper. Not even close. You touched the seal and now they're coming for you. They'll do whatever it takes to get close to you. Always be on your guard, and make no mistake, they can sound like anyone you know or love." And just like that, he was gone.

Chapter Nine

Morning came, and I didn't move. I stayed wrapped up in my blanket, staring at the ceiling like it might offer some kind of clarity. I kept hoping it would take the weight off my chest and ease some of the anxiety and paranoia I have now diagnosed myself with. But it didn't.

There was no way I was going to be able to go back to sleep after he left. In all the chaos, I didn't realize he did not even tell me his name. He just came over, uninvited, to tell me that he knew my father, made a promise to protect me, and that I was in danger.

Once the sun came peaked through my window, I got up, dressed, hopped into my car and started driving. There was only one place where I felt the answers might be hiding. My dad's belongings. Most of it had been boxed up after he died and shoved into a storage unit my mom drunkenly forgot about the second the key hit her hand.

I have not been back in several years, but it feels like the only place in the world where something might make sense. After driving for several hours, I finally make it. I tried calling Miriam and Velicity to let them know I wouldn't be coming in today, but neither of them answered, so I sent them each a quick text with a vague explanation and walked up to the unit.

I stared at the door, trying to decide if I'm happy I thought to make a spare key when mom was passed out drunk one of many times, or if I regretted doing it now. Pushing those thoughts aside, I unlocked the unit door and took a deep breath.

The metal roll-up door creaked open, groaning like it didn't want to be disturbed. Dust clouded the air, and boxes are stacked all around the room. I had no idea what I was even looking for, but I did know where to start. I looked through all the boxes until I found the one I was searching for. I found it at the bottom of a stack in the middle of the room. I dust it off until I was able to read my own handwriting, labeled, "Books & Bibles". Most of it is what I expected. Tattered theology articles, Bible commentaries, and old seminary notes.

However, I came across a Bible that was sealed in a Ziploc bag. It was leather bound but wore out. Unzipping it, a folded envelope slid out from the pages. Inside is a torn journal page, dated two months before he died.

They said she wouldn't remember;
that the veil would hold until the time came.

But the nightmares are starting.
The ash is showing up again.

I think they're circling her already.
She's not safe. And I'm running out of time.

He hasn't answered me in weeks.
If he doesn't come soon,

I'll warn her myself.

I read it twice. And a third time. I didn't want to stop reading but I've read it so much, I have it memorized. Tears threatened to rise, and sadness consumed me, but I swallowed it and kept digging. I always thought my dad was a crazy Bible thumper, but I admired him for sticking to his beliefs. He hadn't been crazy at all, but he had been scared, not of death, but of whatever was coming after me.

Near the bottom of a crate labeled "misc." I found one of his old journals. The spine was cracked and most of the entries were dated years before he died.

The handwriting grew more frantic toward the end. Crossed out lines and rewritten prayers and possible warnings. It's hard to make out, and it makes my heart hurt that my dad was so scared, but seeing his fear in this way makes it even harder.

One page stopped me cold. Scrawled between the margins, between two verses he had scribbles of Psalms, it read:

Azrin. Fallen-but loyal.

He doesn't speak often. Only when the veil thins. But he warned me she was marked.

That she was Chosen.

I can't decide if I can trust him. But I do believe he fears worse than himself.

"Azrin." The word felt strange to say, almost like something sacred I wasn't supposed to know, but without a doubt it was him, the one keeping the darkness at bay.

I closed the journal gently, holding it like it might break, or reveal something I wasn't ready for. Which honestly, at this point, why should anything surprise me anymore?

I closed the lids back on the boxes and totes, then walked out of the unit. I closed the door and turned the lock. The drive home was quiet. I didn't turn on the radio, I just listened to the sounds of the tires on the road and doing what I could to ignore, well, everything.

When I got home, everything was as I left it, but the second I stepped into the kitchen, I knew something was wrong. The air was cooler, and the scent was off. I could smell metal and ash.

I stood there in the doorway, heart racing, and my eyes scanning everywhere. That's when I saw it. My bedroom light was on. I never leave lights on.

Panic was on the verge of wrapping me in its arms and swallowing me whole, but I couldn't let it. I backed out of the kitchen slowly, making sure to avoid the spots in the old floor that creak. When I was back outside, I jumped in my car and tore out of the driveway. I drove three blocks away and parked under a streetlight.

Someone was just in my house, and I didn't believe it was Azrin.

Chapter Ten

I stayed there all night long. Wide awake, debating on going to the police or not. I can see how this drove my dad crazy. It makes my heart ache for him.

One thing was for sure, my house was no longer safe, and quite honestly, neither was pretending I could do this on my own. I needed help. By sunrise, I knew where I needed to go. My father's church, Ashaven Chapel. The irony of the name is not lost on me whatsoever.

He preached there for nearly a decade before everything fell apart. I haven't stepped foot in that place since his funeral, but if he left anything behind, maybe it'll still be there.

The parking lot was empty when I arrived. The chapel itself looked smaller now. I went ahead to walked to the side entrance, the front doors were always locked if it's not a Wednesday or a Sunday. The side entrance was unlocked, like it always used to be. The sanctuary was dark and quiet. Dust danced in the light slicing through the stained glass.

I moved toward the hall behind the pulpit, where my dad's old office was. It hadn't been his in several years, and yet his name is still on the door. **Pastor Daniel Hayes.** I reached for the knob, and it turned with a soft click. Inside, the air was stale, and there were papers stacked everywhere.

I made my way to the desk and opened drawer after drawer. To my surprise I did find something. A file folder, stuffed between two manila envelopes. I opened it and my heart skipped. Inside were pages filled with symbols. Some were drawn in red ink, and some were burned into the paper. At the bottom of one page, three words written in heavy ink:

The Remnant Endures

And below it, a list of names. Except most of them were blacked out. All but one. Eliar Grange. Beside his name read, *Chapelkeeper. Charleston.*

Before I could process any of it, a knock came from somewhere in the church. I froze. Then it came again. I ease out of the office, folder gripped tightly in my hand, and when I get to the sanctuary, I hear a familiar voice on the other side of the doors.

"Piper? Honey, are you int there? It's Mom." My blood went ice cold. My mother never called me honey. I haven't spoken to her since the other day on the phone. Oh crap. Was that even my mother on the phone?

I stayed frozen in place. "It's Mom." The voice repeated. But it wasn't. The voice sounded like hers sure, but it was wrong in all the ways that mattered. "Piper," she said again, "I just want to talk, baby. I've missed you." Something scraped deep in my chest, because for a second, just one traitorous second, I wanted to believe it was her. I took one step forward. That's all it took.

The lights started flickering, and the air dropped ten degrees– that's when a hand gripped my wrist. I spun to only be face to face with Azrin. His face, sharp with fury, and his voice was laced with something worse. "That's not your mother."

I staggered back; breath caught in my throat. The sanctuary doors creaked open just an inch. Just enough to show a sliver of pale skin. Long and pale fingers curled around the edge of the door, and the sight was enough to make me choke on a scream. It didn't even look human.

Azrin moved in front of me, one hand raised. "This place is still marked," he yelled coldly, toward the set of doors. "You can't cross the threshold. You know that."

There was a hiss, sharp and inhuman, and then there was silence, and the door shut on its own.

Azrin didn't turn around. "I told you they would try to sound familiar." He stated. "You're lucky I got here in time."

I wanted to say something. Anything. But the words wouldn't come.

Chapter Eleven

Azrin didn't speak as we left the chapel. I followed him into the parking lot, my heart still pounding and my thoughts raced so loudly, my brain felt like it might explode.

At least I finally knew his name. "Azrin," I said, my voice catching. He didn't look at me, but he paused for a moment, tilting his head without saying anything. "That's you, isn't it?"

He nodded once, "Once upon a time." I took the chance to observe him in the daylight. He was broad-shouldered, lean, and moved with a quiet confidence. His dark hair was tousled in a way that seemed effortless, but I'd bet he spent a lot of time perfecting it. A black leather jacket hugged his frame, and just under his collar of his black t-shirt, I can make out the edges of tattoos.

His piercing green eyes held a steady kind of intensity, with equal parts mystery and danger. Everything about this man radiated a sense of power and respect, palpable in the air around us. He was a frighteningly beautiful man.

Something snapped me to reality, and I realized I had been quietly observing him for longer than I intended. "Well, what does that mean?" I asked, frustration creeping into my voice. He didn't answer, he just kept walking.

I let out a frustrated breath. "You know what? No. You don't get to avoid questions anymore. My whole life just got turned upside down again, after I had finally found some kind of normalcy after years of trying." Tears threatened to break through. Why am I so freaking emotional these days? "Not to mention, I almost opened the door to that thing, even though I knew it wasn't my mom," I said, my voice trembling. "I still felt compelled to let it in. I really would've, if you hadn't shown up."

Azrin's gaze locked onto mine, his expression steady yet irritated. "And that's exactly why I did show up." He replied, irritation lacing his voice. That only made things worse, and I felt the dam holding back my tears crack. A flood of emotions poured out. "Why?" I asked, stepping closer to him. "Why any of this? What did my father get himself into? What exactly am I caught in the middle of?" My voice cracked, and I struggle to hold it together.

Azrin studied me for a long moment, before finally saying, "Your father was part of something a long time ago. They called themselves The Remnant. They believed the veil between worlds wasn't just metaphorical; it was real, and it was fragile. Your father understood this better than anyone, and he knew that you were the key."

I froze. "The key to what?"

He looked away, avoiding my gaze. "Look, I'm just keeping a promise." I let that sit, tears still quietly streaming down my face. I allowed the silence to stretch between us for a moment before speaking again. "I found a name in this file– Someone from the Remnant. Eliar Grange. It says he was a chapel keeper. Does that mean anything to you?" He took a deep breath and looked up at the sky. "If you found that so easily," he said quietly, "anyone can too. And someone far more knowledgeable about this world, will probably discover more."

I stared at him, wiping the tears away– and no doubt leaving mascara streaks on my sleeve. I take a deep breath, unsettled by the way he said that. It almost sounded like he thought that's what was happening. Anger builds inside of me. I have had enough of my life being in danger, albeit a short period of time, and of not knowing any more than I do. "You think they're coming too, don't you?" Azrin didn't answer. He simply stared at the chapel, the wind tugging at the corners of his leather jacket. "Azrin, who *are* they?" I pressed, unable to hide the pleading tone in my voice. "Why are they coming after me and what do they want from me?"

His jaw tightened, "They're what happens when you lose your faith– when you keep feeding the dark even when you know better. They weren't born evil; they chose it. Again and again, until there was nothing left but an uncontrollable, insatiable hunger for the severely depressed."

He looked back at me, "Now they want power. Dominion. And when you touched that seal, you made it known that you are the doorway. You confirmed your existence when, before, the Hollow Ones could only speculate." Those words echoed in the space between us, and felt a wave of nausea wash over me.

I glanced down at my palm. The mark wasn't glowing anymore, but I could still feel its weight pressing down on me. Suddenly, I snapped my eyes at Azrin, and he almost looked startled. A thought hit me hard, like a wrecking ball straight into my chest.

"If they were once people," I said slowly, "does that mean...they still are?" Azrin didn't respond right away. His expression shifted to one of solemnity and sadness.

My stomach twisted. "My mom," I whispered, under the realization that she succumbed to her depression years ago. "Could she be a–?"

He looked away but said, "Some of them are too far gone. What's left isn't human anymore. Not really."

"But not all of them," I pressed. "There's still someone in there, isn't there?"

His voice was quiet, "Sometimes, yes. But that's what can make them so dangerous."

I didn't how to process that information. I wasn't just afraid of the Hollow Ones; I was terrified of the people I love becoming one. I looked at Azrin, striving to mask my fear with determination. "So, what's next?"

This time, he answered without hesitation. "We go to Eliar. If he's still around, he'll know what we need to do next. And if he's not..." He left the sentence hanging.

I glanced back at Ashaven Chapel one last time, trying to prepare myself for what lies ahead.

Chapter Twelve

Azrin

She didn't ask any more questions when we left the chapel. Instead, she climbed into the passenger seat, pulled her knees up to her chest, and stared out the window like the sky might give her something solid to hold onto. Ashaven faded in the review mirror, and with it, the last piece of safety I'm sure she thought she had.

I felt a pang of sympathy for her, but it was better that she didn't know that. She believed this was the beginning, but she couldn't be further from the truth. The beginning happened long before she was born, when a tear opened in the veil and allowed the wrong things to slip through. Her father knew it. He even tried to fight it and protect her from it.

I glanced over at her after a while, and she appeared to be asleep. Her hand was resting near the edge of the seat, her fingers twitching. I looked away. This is why I didn't get involved. This is why I stopped making promises. Because eventually, they all look like this–small and weak. She was just a human, shouldering the edge of a war she can't even begin to comprehend, one that I've already watched nearly tear everything apart.

But I gave her father my word. And with the seal on her hand and the Hollow Ones following her, I was running out of time to keep it.

Chapter Thirteen

The ride to Charleston was long and quiet. I tried to sleep, but every time I closed my eyes, I could see those fingers -pale and inhuman- curled around the chapel door. Then there was the current problem: I'm in a car with a man I barely knew, and with the string of events that felt too insane to process, I didn't feel comfortable letting my guard down for a second.

I kept my eyes on the window, but I wasn't seeing anything except the sun setting. The silence in the car was heavy. I had a million questions swirling in my mind, but he's made it very clear he isn't going to answer them the way I want.

My thoughts drifted to my mother, and I felt a twinge of guilt. I feel guilty for moving away and letting her succumb further to her demons. I don't know for sure that my mother had turned, or whatever you would call it. I don't even know that whole process or why I'm just now seeing it. My process of elimination pointed to the seal on my hand, and of course, being a veilbreaker—whatever that meant. I didn't like the sound of it, especially since breaking the veil is what landed us here in the first place, at least that's my understanding.

My fingers tightened around the edge of my sweatshirt as I check my phone. No one from the library has reached out to me. I wasn't sure if that was strange or not, considering this was the most I've called into work in the 7 years I've worked there.

Azrin shifted slightly, pulling me from my thoughts. He had one hand on the wheel, the other resting by his side where I just noticed something sticking out from his shirt. It looks like a...hilt? What the heck? Is that a sword? How have I not seen it this whole time? I checked him out earlier and I know that was not there. My mind was spinning. I looked at his face, he looked calm, but I could still see some tension.

"Azrin, what happens if they get me first?" I asked without even consulting myself if I was really prepared for the answer I might get.

He glanced over at me, and I couldn't place an emotion. He looked to be feeling so many, but I could see anger swirling just behind his eyes. I hoped he wasn't angry at me but at the situation. He looked back at the road, his jaw flexed slightly as if he were weighing what to say. Finally, he said, "Then it's all over." I shook my head and smiled a little to myself.

"Well, that's vague." I replied. He was silent once again.

"So, what?" I asked trying to stay levelheaded. "Do they kill me? Possess me? Tear apart my soul and throw a housewarming party in my skin?" Well, that seemed to get his attention.

He snapped his head toward me, fury written all over his face. "Do you think this is a joke?"

"No," I said firmly. "I think I'm a human being who just found out monsters are real, and apparently, the survival of the world rests on my shoulders. Forgive me if sarcasm is my defense mechanism right now." Then another thought crossed my mind: Is Azrin human? He looked like one, but something about him felt different. I made a mental note to ask about that later.

This fool still didn't respond. I waited ten minutes, hoping for something, but nothing came. He's going to regret being in this car with me. "Who are you really?" I asked, finally. "You obviously knew my dad well enough to promise you'd look after his daughter, but I've never seen you. And there weren't many people in our lives. So, who are you Azrin, or should I be asking *what* are you?"

His hands flexed on the steering wheel. He stayed quiet again. Him not telling me something that should be so simple, makes me start to panic. There's something he isn't telling me or doesn't want me to know, and I am not okay with it.

"Dude, who are you? I will roll out of this car right now if you don't answer me." I spew as I fume with anger. Apparently, so is he. His knuckles turned white from gripping the steering wheel so tight. Then, without a word, he turned off the highway. We pulled onto a narrow road surrounded by trees, the pavement giving way to gravel, then to dirt.

"Oh no, seriously?" I said, my voice climbing. The car rolled to a stop, and he cut the engine off. He went to get out and I couldn't control my heart rate or my panic. "You have lost your mind if you think I am getting out of my car with a man I don't know in the woods, where quite literally no one knows where I am." He shut the door and started walking to the woods.

I stayed frozen in my seat, my heart hammering in my chest. This was it. This whole thing has been a lie, a ploy, and now I'm about to be murdered in the woods.

You wanted the truth. I'm going to show you instead of telling you. He spoke crystal clear in my head. I gasped and whipped my head toward my window. He was already entering the trees. Every sane instinct I had screamed not to follow him, but something deeper was tugging me toward him. So, of course, I grabbed the keys out of the ignition and got out.

The woods felt eerie, and each step away from my car was like a hand pressing down on my chest.

When I finally caught up to him, he stood in a small clearing. The moonlight filtered through the trees like fractured glass, giving this situation even more of a 'get out now' feeling.

"You've been begging to know what I am, so I'm going to show you. But after this, things will change. There will be no more doubts, no more questioning me. This is it." He had a dangerous edge to his tone. I pulled my car keys from my pocket in case I needed to make a run for my car.

The air around us changed, the wind picked up a little and the leaves started swirling around us in a circle. I glanced back at him and his shoulders shifted as he took a deep breath, and his spine arched back slightly.

No freaking way. I couldn't breathe. Not because I was afraid, but because he looked absolutely ethereal.

Wings. If the moonlight wasn't shining right on him, you wouldn't even see them. They were the darkest of black. Obsidian is the closest I can describe it.

He turned to face me fully.

Good Lord. He's stunning. His green eyes were piercing in the dark, but they did not look like normal green eyes. They were almost glowing in the dark, but green... My breath caught in my throat, and I couldn't find any words to say.

He broke the silence. "I'm a fallen angel."

Chapter Fourteen

A fallen angel. Like the devil? I have so many questions, but I couldn't manage to open my mouth and make any words come out. My breathing was shallow, and my heart was pounding. The air was still, and even the trees appear to be holding their breath.

Azrin stood just a few feet away, wings stretched out behind him, and he really does look like a force to be reckoned with. Angels are real, which would mean Heaven is real, which would then mean God is real.

My mind was blown. [*I can't even think straight, heck, I can barely think at all. I'm just standing here gawking at him, probably making him feel like a freak.*]

Azrin broke the silence first, "Say something." His voice sounding like a question more than a statement or a demand. He almost sounded unsure, maybe even concerned. I swallowed hard and willed my voice to work. "I thought angel wings would be white. I'm guessing that something to do with you falling?" He didn't answer, and he didn't have to. Now that I was really looking at him, he is a combination of sadness and sorrow. It's almost like its eating him alive, from the inside out, and my heart really does hurt for him.

It's crazy to me that I used to believe in all of this. But that was a different, more innocent version of me. When I lost my father, any kind of faith and hope I ever had died with him. And now here I was, face-to-face with someone I consciously chosen not to believe in. A wave of incredulous guilt washed over me. We watched each other in silence. The shadows of his wings curled slightly, as if reacting to something I couldn't see. Then he spoke, his voice low and his tone laced with a finality I hadn't heard before. "Piper, if you have any questions about me, what I've done, or anything relating to me, this is your chance to ask. You ask them now, or you don't ask them at all." Something defiant within me bristled at being told what to do, especially by a man I barely knew. But the intensity of his tone and the fact that he was an angel kept me from arguing.

My heart pounded. I knew he was rough around the edges, but I didn't expect him to be so harsh, especially now that I know he's an angel. A thousand questions flooded my mind, but one rose to the surface faster than the rest, "Were you in my house the other night? I got home, and someone was there, but I managed to get out without them noticing."

He slowly shook his head. "No, that wasn't me. But you knew that already." He was right about that. "How did I know that? And while we're on that subject, how can you talk in my mind?" He shifted on his feet, rubbing his hands over his face as his gaze drifted past me, weighing how much to reveal. "Ever since I made the promise, a thread connected us. It was faint enough I could always find you if I needed to. But when you touched the seal, well it sealed the promise, and it changed."

"Changed how?" I pressed, my curiosity piqued.

He took a step closer. "It bound us. I can feel you no matter where you are, I can feel your emotions, and you can do the same for me. It's how you knew it wasn't me in your house that night. You'll sense me before you ever see me." He watched me carefully, like he was watching how I was handling the information. Taking another step forward, "The connection also allows us into each other's minds." *Which is how I'm able to do this.* I felt my eyes widen. I took a step back without meaning to. Well, crap. So, he can read my mind and heard all the things I've thought about him since meeting him.

The corner of his mouth turned up slightly. "Okay, that is not okay. You can't just invade my privacy like that." I stumble to take another step back, and I backed myself right against a tree. He kept coming closer, slowly and carefully, giving me time to protest or make a move to distance us.

"You keep asking me questions and I told you I'd answer them, and I have. But make no mistake, I swore to protect you, and that's what I'm going to do. No matter what." His hand lifted, but not in a threat, but in the kind of way that makes you forget what's going on around you. His fingers brushed the side of my face, like he was being careful to not hurt me.

The moment his skin touched mine, I wasn't in the woods anymore. I was somewhere else entirely. The world around me shimmered, the sound warped like I was underwater, and then a single image finally came into focus.

A boy.

No, *the* boy. The one in my dreams, but older. Maybe even closer to my age. Standing in the middle of the burnt field, the broken altar behind him, and the smoke curling from the ground. He smiled when he saw me, not a happy smile, but one of recognition.

Then– it was darkness. I opened my eyes to find myself lying on the ground, moonlight emphasizing an ethereal glow on Azrin's face. He cradled my face with both of his hands, his eyes searching mine frantically.

"Piper," he said, urgency coating his voice. "What's wrong? What happened?"

My breath hitched and I tried to regain my bearings. I blinked hard and noticed that my hands were shaking. I wiped away a tear I hadn't realize had formed. I explained to him and even went as far to tell him about my dreams and nightmares, whatever you want to call them.

Azrin's jaw tightened. Suddenly, I was overwhelmed with anger, helplessness, and guilt. It took me a moment to realize that they weren't my emotions, they were his.

"What's wrong, Azrin?" His eyes flicked away. He stood, tension winding through him. A long pause. "He's the boy I couldn't save." The air felt like it shattered around us. "I think you keep dreaming of him because you're tied to him. His blood runs in your veins."

My head spun and felt like it's going to explode. "What are you talking about?" I whispered.

His gaze finally met mine again, and I knew what he was going to say before he said it, "You're a descendant of the boy I failed," he said. "That's why you're seeing him." A heavy silence followed. My breath caught at the confirmation of what I was anticipating him to say. The weight of the words knocked the air from my chest.

Then he continued, his voice quieter, like the memory itself was almost too painful to talk about. "I made a promise to myself after I lost him. That if I ever had the chance to make it right, I would do it. I didn't know how. I just knew

I would do whatever it took." He stepped closer, his voice steady, but rough.

"Years passed. And then your father found me." I blinked at him. I started to feel dizzy at the knowledge, and I have no words to say at the moment.

Thankfully, Azrin continued, "He knew who I was through someone in the Remnant. He knew that I had failed massively, and he still looked me in the eye, explained his situation and who you were, and that he felt it in his gut you were the one to rise from the ashes, in a metaphorical sense." It was like a wall that Azrin spent years building to hide his emotions, had crumbled and he was letting it all free.

With the connection to each other I could feel his guilt and his regret, but I could also feel relief. I begin to wonder how long it had been since he had a friend, or just someone to confide in.

Taking a deep breath and continued, "Your father had no doubt that you were the key to ending the impending war should you choose to. But he made it very clear that it had to be your choice."

My heart was thundering, and I could feel my hands trembling. He held my gaze, "So I made the promise to your father. And I know that I said I was here because of that and not because of you. But I'm here for you too." He had so many emotions running through him, they were starting to overwhelm me on top of my own emotions I was trying to sort through.

Something in his eyes shifted, they were no longer guarded, but pleading, "I'm here to try to convince you to help save a world that I believe is worth saving."

Chapter Fifteen

For what felt like a long time, I didn't say anything. Azrin's words hung in the space between us like thick smoke. I'm still trying to digest everything he shared with me. The biggest thought being he thinks this world is worth saving, and he wants *me* to help save it.

I looked to my right, my gaze catching on the trees surrounding us. The woods were quiet and still, and it felt like they were watching us, or watching me at least.

The weight I'm feeling on my shoulders is indescribable. I'm just a woman who came from a traumatic past and only believed in God because I was supposed to and because my dad did. But then I stopped when he died because it hurt, and I didn't feel like I had a reason to.

How can I sit here and say the same thing to be true when I'm in the presence of a real-life angel, fallen or not, he's real and he's tangible.

"I don't know that I can do this," I admitted quietly. I looked back at him and he just nodded once. "I know you don't feel that way now, but the fact that you didn't immediately say no says everything about you." Something in me fills with pride and I almost immediately recognize it as Azrin.

"I'm not asking you to be ready, I'm only asking if you're willing to try and to take the steps necessary to be at your best and to give this your best shot." I hung my head between my knees, making myself breathe and try to regulate my heartbeat. He moved suddenly, causing me to look up at him, he had turned like he was listening for something.

"We should get moving." He said with the slightest tone of urgency. I stood up and brushed myself off. He started moving in the direction we came, when I grabbed his arm. "Azrin, what happens now?" I asked in a faint whisper.

He looked at my hand and then back at me. "Right now, we just need to find the Remnant. See if we can find any more pertinent information, and then we will reassess."

I dropped my hand from his arm, and he started back to my car. I followed behind him, but not too closely. The silence between us stretched thin as we walked back. The moon hung low, casting shadows that felt heavier now. My thoughts are still tangled in everything Azrin had said.

When we make it to the car, Azrin stood at the passenger door like he was waiting for something. I stopped walking and looked at him. I didn't even notice his wings were gone. I make a mental note to ask him about that later, when he interrupted my thoughts by clearing his throat. I turn my attention back to him, and he nodded toward the car.

Oh, yeah. I have the keys. Not realizing I was still clutching them; I handed them to him. He unlocked it and opened my door for me. I slid into the passenger seat and stared out the window. Azrin got in the driver seat and put the key in the ignition but for some reason, he hesitated to start the car.

"They're not just coming for you, Piper. They want full dominion. Not just of the world, but of everything. If the breach the boundary, if they infect enough souls, they'll tip the balance, and Heaven will have no choice but to respond."

I slowly turned my head and found him gazing at me with fear and anger mixed in his gaze. My heart dropped and my pace quickened. "What are you saying to me, Azrin?" not trying to hide the panic in my voice, knowing full well he can feel my emotions.

He took a deep breath before responding. "I'm saying this isn't just about you. The fact that the veil is already torn means that people have been succumbing to their own darknesses and choosing to continue to live in sin, which means the Hollow Ones are ahead of us already."

He studied my face for a moment, adding, "It's the century old battle of demons against angels, or good versus evil. But this would be the last battle, because you're the last Veilbreaker."

I swallowed hard, "So, if I do decide to say no.."

He looked ahead through the windshield, "If you say no then decent humans don't stand a chance, and when the impending war does come, which it will and much sooner if they don't have your help, then sin and darkness will run rampant. There will be no faith, no hope, and no religion. You can go ahead and chalk it up to being the end of the world."

I didn't have words for such heavy weight. I was just a woman with a fractured past, sitting with a fallen angel, and the weight of holding the fate of both Heaven and Earth in my shaking hands.

And I wasn't sure which scared me more, the weight I've been given, or the part of me that was starting to believe I was meant to carry it.

Chapter Sixteen

Azrin

Not one word was spoken from her in over a hundred miles. I disliked putting all of that on her, and that's not at all how I intended on doing it, but time is running out.

I glance at her out of the corner of my eye. She's curled against the door, face half-hidden in the glow of the passing streetlights. Her expression is unreadable, but the silence tells me all I need to know. She's trying to hold her whole world together after it's been split wide open. I've seen that look before and have even worn it myself.

For the first time in a long time, I don't know what to do with the weight of someone else's pain. Truth is, I should've never gotten this close. Ever since I made the promise with her father, I've always kept my distance. I would go days without checking on her.

I have been keeping tabs on the demons and the darkness and nothing really stood out to me too much regarding the veil and Piper. Until I felt the burn in the palm of my hand, branding me with the Remnant symbol. Everything shifted, I could feel her. The connection between us locking into place, ancient and binding. And now, I can't walk away, but not because of the oath I made, but because of her.

She's the answer to everything. The Hollow Ones grow more desperate by the day, and she is their main target. If they get to her... *I can't even finish that thought.* I grip the wheel harder.

I look back at her. She's absolutely phenomenal. Her hair is long, straight, and as black as my wings. She wears glasses that frame her face perfectly. After watching her over the years, I've learned a thing or two about her, and I can honestly say there's not a bad thing I could say about her.

She has a big heart despite everything she's gone through. She loves animals, she's kind to people she doesn't know, and the thing that stands out the most to me, is that even though she hasn't been religious since her father passed, she still takes care to not curse or lead a life blatantly deep with sin. I can't decide if that's on purpose or if it's because it's a habit that her father instilled in her.

She's one of a kind, and I'll die protecting her. The world needs her, they need more of her.

I turn my attention back to the road, hoping and praying that I'm not driving into a storm that I can't outrun.

Chapter Seventeen

I did not remember falling asleep, but I must have at some point during the duration of the drive. When I open my eyes, sunlight beamed through the windshield. The sky is pale and overcast, and the hum of the road beneath us was steady.

Azrin's hand was on the wheel and the is other resting near the gearshift. He hasn't noticed I'm awake, or maybe he has and he's giving me the chance to say something first. Either way, I take a second to breathe in the quiet before I speak.

"My stomach may actually eat itself," I murmur.

His gaze flicks over to me, "Well, good morning. There's a diner about ten miles out. It's nothing fancy but the food is good." He shifted in his seat, "You fell asleep around four and I didn't want to bother you, so I didn't stop. I figured you needed rest more than food."

I sat up straighter, rubbing my hands down my thighs. "Those aren't exactly the best caretaker instincts. Women need food more than sleep, at least this woman does."

He huffs a quiet breath that I almost think might turn into a laugh. "I'm not a caretaker, Piper. I'm just...keeping my promise." I study him. There's something behind that statement. Something heavier than he's letting on.

"Does it feel like a burden?" I ask, my voice softer. "Keeping that promise?"

He doesn't answer right away. When he does speak, it's barely louder than a whisper. "It did," he admits. "For a long time. Until I met you." That lands harder than I expected it to. I swallow, unsure of what to say.

"I don't know what I'm doing," I say quietly, turning toward the window. "All of this, it feels too big for me."

"You're allowed to be scared, Piper." He says. "But don't ever confuse fear with weakness."

I glance back at him. "Careful, you sound like you might actually believe in me." I was partially joking and partially serious.

He looked at me with a softness I hadn't seen from him yet and then I could feel his pride, warm and steady. "I wouldn't be here if I didn't."

Azrin pulled into a dusty parking lot beside a weathered little diner with a flickering neon sign that read "**Lula's**". The place looked like it hadn't changed since the 80's, but the smell of bacon and coffee cut through the air like a promise.

I made a squeak and did a little excited dance, already reaching for the door. I can't even remember the last time I ate. He gave a small chuckle and got out himself. He stretched a bit and then held the door to the diner open for me.

Inside, the diner was quiet, a soft hum of an old jukebox played in the corner and there was a clatter of dishes. A waitress with silver hair and tired eyes gave us a polite smile and motioned to a booth in the back.

We slid in across from each other. I knew I was hungry, I just didn't realize how hungry until I smelled the food. "Piper," Azrin said once we were settled, his voice low. "I know it feels like you have to bear this alone. But you don't, I want to help you in any way I can."

I nod my head appreciatively. "Thank you, Azrin. That means a lot. Honestly, I just want to know what's happening to me, and what's happening around me."

A silence stretched between us, heavy, but not uncomfortable. Then I looked up at him and asked, "What did the world look like the last time something like this happened?" His expression shifted to a grim, sad look, "It looked like ash and ruin."

Swallowing. "Do you think it'll come to that again?" He reached for a menu and then he met my gaze, "Not if you stop it. You're different than the other veilbreakers. You've got the stubbornness, and the passion needed to get the job done. Should you choose to."

Changing the subject for a minute, I looked over the menu. "I think I'm going to order half of the menu." Azrin laughed, like actually belly laughed and it was the greatest sound I think I've ever heard.

"You just had your whole life wrecked, so I think you should do whatever makes your heart happy." Yep, that was the right answer.

The food came fast, and we both dug in like it had been days since we last ate. And it probably has been. For a moment, everything feels normal. The clink of the silverware, the low buzz of conversation around us, it made me almost forget what we were running from.

Until the air shifted.

I have become familiar with that shift in the environment. It's a slight, subtle drop in temperature. Azrin's posture changed before I even spoke. One of his hands was resting flat on the table, both of his shoulders tense. "You feel it too," he asked me every inch of his voice laced with anger. I nodded slowly.

Out of the corner of my eye, I saw a shadow behind the counter. I kept my eyes focused on Azrin trying to keep my emotions in check so they didn't overwhelm him, and he could think clearly. In my peripheral, I could barely make out their appearances. They were just tall figures cloaked in something that shimmered like smoke.

The odd thing to me was that no one else in the diner even seemed perturbed by them. No one even looked in the direction of the figures or even seemed to notice they were there.

I whispered to Azrin, "No one can see them, can they? Why can I?"

'Because, Azrin started to say in my mind, *"you're not unaware of the war anymore, you're a crucial part of it. When you touched the seal on your dad's journal, you opened the door that allows you to see the supernatural."*

A dark movement to my left made me turn my head and the Hollow Ones had started to move. My fingers clenched into fists on my lap, and I felt the prickling burn of fear along my spine. Azrin stood without a sound. He didn't draw attention. No one in the diner even acknowledged him or looked our way.

He reached behind him, and when he moved again, there was a long blade in his hand. It was silver-edged, and humming with an energy that I could almost feel in my bones. He muttered something under his breath that

I couldn't make out. That's when the Hollow Ones surged forward. I had only noticed two originally and suddenly a third came out of nowhere.

The first one lunged, and Azrin moved like lightning. I'd never seen anything like it. One second, he was standing next to me, and the next he was in front of the booth intercepting the strike. His blade collided with the creature, and a burst of smoky light exploded on impact, sending a ripple through the diner that still no one noticed.

Azrin fought with precision and fury, but the Hollow Ones didn't stop. More kept appearing, before I knew it there were seven. I felt so helpless. One of them flanked Azrin, slipping past his blade, and that was it. I didn't think, I just moved.

"Piper, NO!"

But it was too late. I threw myself forward, pushing Azrin out of the way just as the Hollow One's clawed hand came swinging down. Pain ripped through my side, hot and sharp. I heard myself cry out, but the sound felt far away.

Azrin's voice roared, but I couldn't hold on.

That's when I fell and everything blurred.

Chapter Eighteen

Azrin

Blood soaked through the side of her shirt, warm and dark. My hands shook as I pressed them to the wound, trying to stop what I already knew I couldn't. Her skin had gone pale; her breaths were shallow.

"Piper." Her name came out as a sob, desperate and broken. She didn't answer.

A sound tore from my throat, raw and inhuman. The Hollow Ones froze—just for a moment. But it was enough. I carefully placed Piper's body in the booth behind me. Then I turned.

I lost control.

The blade in my hand burned with power. My wings unfurled behind me in a violent snap of air. The Hollow Ones flinched, and a smile broke across my face. The first one came at me again. I drove my sword through its chest. Light exploded from the wound like fire catching on oil, and it shrieked before disintegrating.

Another lunged. I grabbed it with both hands and *ripped* it apart, smoke and ash raining down. They kept coming. Stronger than they've ever been. They were feeding on the darkness surging through the world, growing stronger by the second.

I fought like a storm that was finally unleashed. Not for vengeance. Not for redemption. But for her.

For the woman so selfless, she jumped in front of a blade intended for a fallen angel.

The last enemy had snuck behind me while I was distracted with another and got too close to her. I nearly lost it again. I launched myself forward, slicing through its neck and sending its shriveled head rolling beneath the counter before it disintegrated into a pile of ash.

My body ached, and I could feel my power waning. Just then, the door to the diner opened, setting off the bell at the top and pulling me from my thoughts. A gust of cold wind rolled in, and with it came Eliar.

He walked closer, standing beside me with an unsettling calmness. "Looks like I got here just in time," he said matter-of-factly. I ignored him and rushed over to Piper. Eliar followed and crouched down beside me.

"They're getting stronger," he murmured under his breath, like I didn't just figure that out for myself. "They will keep coming for her. Every chance they get."

Anger boiled inside me, a fire I had never felt before. I clenched my jaw, "She stepped in front of me." Eliar let out a slow breath and gave me a pat on the shoulder.

"Of course she did. She's special." For a moment, we just sat there in the diner's eerie stillness, surrounded by people who had no idea the world had just come a little closer to unraveling and possibly ending if they had succeeded in killing Piper.

Eliar reached out, pressed two fingers lightly to Piper's wrist. His brow furrowed, then relaxed slightly. "She'll live," he said. "But not if we stay here."

"I'll carry her." The words came out sharp, clipped. I cleared my throat. Eliar studied me for a moment, then nodded. He rose and took a step toward the door. "Then let's move."

I looked around the diner. The patrons sat oblivious—sipping coffee, scrolling phones, existing in their bubble of normalcy and peace. Piper would save every one of them without hesitation. I knew that about her. But the question that gnawed at me now was sharper than a blade: At what cost?

Chapter Nineteen

The first thing I noticed was pain— a dull, dragging ache pulsed through my side, as though something heavy had lodged itself there and refused to let go. The second was warmth. Solid. Real. Someone's chest.

I blinked repeatedly, fighting the blur. The world came back in patches; the low rumble of a car engine, sunlight bleeding through the windshield, the reminder that the world hadn't stopped just because mine had shattered.

Azrin.

I didn't have to look to know. His presence pressed around me like a shield— fraying at the edges with tension. He was holding me, cradling me like I might break.

A breath shuddered through me, and my ribs caught fire. I winced.

"Piper." His voice was gravel and restraint. "Don't move. We need to see how much damage was done."

"What ha...?" My voice cracked, the words fragmenting. Talking made everything worse. "You passed out," he said, softer now. "One of the Hollow Ones got too close while I was distracted. You took the hit for me."

I didn't respond right away. I wasn't sure I could. The memory came back in flashes—the worst being Azrin's face after it happened. "Is everyone okay?" I asked, because I needed to know. "The people in the diner?"

"They never even noticed," he replied. "You were the only one who saw the fight for what it really was." I closed my eyes and nodded. Then opened them again. "Where are we going?"

"To someone who can help with your wound," Azrin answered, but his grip on me tightened—a subtle shift I definitely noticed. I shifted, ignoring the pain. "You were going to die back there."

He didn't answer. He didn't need to. The silence said everything. Of course he would die.

That was the promise. That was the whole reason. But lately... I wondered if it had become something more.

Azrin looked down at me, his jaw set. "They were going to kill you."

My heart quickened. I was suddenly hyperaware of everything—how close I had come to never seeing him again. How close he had come to letting me.

"You were going to let them kill you first," I whispered. He didn't deny it.

"You can't keep doing that, Azrin." I whispered. His grip tightened on me again, this time he didn't try to hide it.

I looked up at him and placed my hand on his cheek and guided him to look at me.

"I'm not worth losing you."

Azrin didn't answer. He just looked at me- really looked at me. Then slowly, he leaned in and rested his forehead against mine. The warmth of the gesture sent something trembling through my chest. It was gentle and sweet. I closed my eyes and just reveled in the moment. It felt so normal.

Until it dawned on me. We are in the backseat, so who is driving?

"Azrin," I pulled back slightly, eyes scanning the small space around us. "Whose driving?"

He pushed my hair behind my ear and said, "Eliar." I just blinked at him.

"The Remnant tracks the Hollow Ones, so he was tracking the ones that attacked us. He's a friend, well sometimes. He's really an impossible person. You'll see."

I guess the look on my face was funny because this time he gave me a full, ear to ear smile. "We've known each other a long time. He keeps what's left of the Remnant together, and I help with the Hollow Ones occasionally when they need it.

"You help them?" Skepticism crept into my voice. I just always assumed Azrin didn't know anyone because of how mysterious he is. He looked behind me, at Eliar I'm assuming. I want to look at him but the pain in my side is preventing me from doing a whole lot of moving. I'll be glad when we get there, wherever "there" is.

"Of course. Let's just say we have a mutual interest in keeping the veil intact. Not to mention keeping you alive and safe."

My stomach twisted and the reminder weighed on me hard. I haven't felt like a burden until now. Azrin must've noticed the change in my expression, because his face softened and he said, "You're safe. You're okay."

A voice from behind me called out, deep, gritty, and country? "I can hear everything y'all are saying and I feel like it's about time we got properly introduced." I had to keep my composure because I sure didn't expect a member of the Remnant to sound like that. I do not know what I was expecting to be honest, but I do know it wasn't that.

Azrin sighed and smirked, "Piper, meet Eliar. Eliar, meet Piper- the girl you're not allowed to let die."

Eliar made a huffing sound and said, "Actually, my friend, you're the one not allowed to let her die. I personally like living and just have a vested interest in keeping it that way." He laughed and it was a beautiful sound. It was contagious and it made me smile wide.

I leaned into Azrin's shoulder and watched the world go by through the window, and something in me finally let go. The heaviness I'd been carrying for so long, since my dad passed honestly, began to lift. Just a little, but enough for me to breathe easier.

For the first time, I wasn't facing anything alone.

Chapter Twenty

We rode the rest of the way in silence. I kept dozing off; the pain in my side made it hard to focus on anything else, but it didn't hurt as long as I was asleep. By the time we pulled off the main road, the sun was dipping in the horizon, staining the sky with hues of orange and bruised violet. We turned down a gravel road lined with towering trees that swallowed the last of the light.

Azrin's hand brushed against mine. "We're almost there." He said softly, his in turmoil. I had learned that if I just looked at him and concentrated just enough, I could feel his feelings and his emotions– a wild ability I was still trying to comprehend.

The trees opened into a clearing, revealing a chapel covered in ivy, the most ancient-looking building I had ever seen. To be honest, it looked creepy. The steeple leaned to the left, and the stained-glass windows desperately needed cleaning.

Eliar rolled the car to a stop and put it in park. He got out and jogged to the passenger back door and opened it for us. He helped get me out as easily as he could and when I threw my arm over his shoulder and he put his arm around my waist, I heard a low and dangerous...growl? Oh yeah, that is definitely a growl. I was then filled with anger and jealousy.

I snapped my head to the side and Azrin is looking at Eliar like he wanted to rip him apart. I cannot even.

"Are you freaking kidding me? Eliar, stop for just one second." Eliar halted and looked at Azrin, confusion etched on his face.

"Oh, good gracious. I don't have the time to play these crazy games with you, boy. Get over here and take my place if it'll calm your horses." Azrin moved quickly, taking his place and lifting me into a fireman carry.

I roll my eyes. "Azrin, put me down. I can walk and I *want* to walk." He took a deep breath, almost like he was pouting, and reluctantly placed me on my feet. Once he had his arm around my waist supporting me, he was extra careful to avoid my wound, he started walking towards the chapel.

As we approached, I noticed a symbol carved into the door– the same one on my hand and in my dad's journal. The moment I walked by it, the mark shimmered. This was all so surreal, and I can't believe this is my life right now.

Inside, candlelight flickered from sconces on the stone walls. It smelled like dust and wood. Eliar opened a second door for us to the left of the altar. "We've got beds and supplies in the back." Then he looked at me and smiled, "And there's at least one working toilet." He gave me a wink that made me smile. But it also made me wonder when the last time I had even peed was.

Azrin helped me settle onto one of the worn cots. My legs felt shaky and my eyes felt heavy the instant I laid down. I slept on and off in the car, but I guess it wasn't enough.

"I'll go get you something to eat," Azrin said, turning to head back out the door. My heart swells at how thoughtful he was being.

"Azrin," I said quickly. "What is this place?" He turned back around. "It's one of the safehouses the Remnant has," he explained. "It's sanctified ground, which just means its protected and the Hollow Ones can't enter. But they will still try to lure someone out, as you've already learned."

He walked over to a corner and lit another candle, his silhouette danced in the soft glow. I leaned back, my eyes scanned the cracked ceiling above me. Every time I thought I had reached my limit, something else peels back another layer. I close my eyes, attempting to calm my breathing which I hadn't realized had quickened.

Suddenly, a voice– raspy and low– filled the room. "Where is she?" My eyes snapped open, and I lift my head, wincing at the pain in my side. Standing near the doorway was a woman in a dark cloak, eyes so gray they looked like smoke. "She's stronger than the others," The woman said, directing her words to Azrin.

"The veil has thinned even more. She needs to be ready."

Azrin crossed the room in two steps, his jaw clenched. "Let her rest and heal."

"We don't have the time," the woman stated simply. She turned to me. "Rest tonight. Tomorrow, you learn what it means to be a Veilbreaker." She vanished as suddenly as she appeared.

I sat up too quickly, pain searing through my side like a knife dragging across my skin. I sucked in a breath, pressing my hand to the wound.

Azrin was by my side in a heartbeat. "We have got to get you stitched up," he muttered, his voice rough with worry.

"You don't say," I winced. He knelt in front of me, lifting the hem of my shirt gently. "Hold still." His fingers were careful yet warm and calloused. I took a deep breath as he rolled my shirt up slightly, just enough to have access to my side and not a centimeter higher.

He dipped a cloth into a bowl of steamy water– someone must've placed there while I wasn't paying attention– he carefully dabbed my side. I hissed through my teeth.

"Well, the good news is, it's not any deeper than it is. It's going to heal just fine, but it will leave a scar." He said concerningly. I didn't know what to say to that, so I didn't say anything. He worked on my side in silence for a little while. Then he sighed, "You scared me to death." I looked at him. I hadn't noticed the scar on his right cheek before.

Something between us was changing. He was no longer the stranger who creeped me out by following me around or the man who was keeping a promise to my father. He was becoming the person I look to for an answer or reassurance– essentially for everything. Quickly remembering that he can feel my emotions and read my thoughts, I shifted my focus to save the embarrassment.

"Who was that woman?" I asked quietly. Azrin sat back on his heels, glancing toward the door where the cloaked figure had earlier stood. "Her name is Maeryn. She's what is commonly known as an Oracle–well as close as a person can get to it." He rubbed a hand through his hair, "She's a very reclusive person and only shows herself when things get desperately bad."

I breathed a laugh, "And things are bad." I noted.

He nodded, "Worse than I thought. If she's here, it means the Veil is weaker than it's ever been."

His expression darkened. "You're not just able to see the Hollow Ones, Piper. You're drawing them in, attracting them. You may not think you have faith or believe in God anymore, but they can feel it and they know it's thin. The closer you get to your faith, the harder it will be for them to corrupt you. They will continue to try," he looked at me hopeful, "but it'll be easier for you to keep your mind intact."

I lay back down, giving myself space to absorb his words. He moved back in position to finish up with my wound. When he was done, he didn't pull away. He just stayed there, kneeling beside me with something like awe in his eyes. He truly was amazing to look at.

"Azrin?" I say softly. His eyes meet mine, "Yes, Piper?"

"I'm glad you aren't letting me face this alone."

He brought his forehead to mine, again. "You were never alone."

Chapter Twenty-One

She stood at the far end of the chapel, beside a wall lined with candles. Dressed in a loose gray sweater and worn jeans, her long white braid hung down her back like a ribbon of silver. When I walked in, she looked at me and smiled.

"Piper Elowen Hayes," she said. I nodded, gave her a small wave, and took a few steps toward her. She motioned for me to sit at a table in front of her. As I reached the table, I noticed a Bible open, its pages soft with wear. There were underlines, notes in the margins, and small strips of paper bookmarking various passages throughout the book.

"You can call me Maeryn, as I'm sure Azrin told you." I nodded again, opening my mouth to speak, but she cut me off. "I just want you to know I know this is all so tough to take in. But I want to make one thing very clear to you." She reached out, and grabbing my hand and looking me in the eye, "God doesn't call the qualified. He qualifies the called." Hearing that broke something in me, and tears began to stream down my face. Before I could stop myself, I was reaching out and pulling her in for a hug.

When we pulled away, she motioned for me to sit beside her. "Do you know what a Veilbreaker is?" she asked. I shook my head, still trying to stop the tears. My throat had a bad habit of closing up when I cry, making it hard to speak.

She traced the verse slowly with one finger. "'The heart of man plans his way, but the Lord establishes his steps.'—Proverbs 16:9. Veilbreakers are spiritual catalysts. They don't just see through the Veil, but they are chosen to help tip the scales. Intended for good to prevail, for God's light to be seen in the world."

I finally managed to take a deep breath and speak. "That sounds terrifying," I whispered.

Looking down at the verse, as her words echoed in my ears. For the first time, I wasn't just afraid; I was *trembling* under the weight of it all. Maeryn stood up. "Follow me."

She led me to a smaller room off the sanctuary. It resembled half a study and half a training room, with books and desks on one side and training dummies, along with various weapons and equipment, on the other side.

"We train body, mind, and spirit here," Maeryn said. "Seeing as you have never been trained in your life, we must begin now."

Training was way harder than I had anticipated. Physically, I was drained, and my side throbbed. Emotionally and mentally, I was just as exhausted. I had no idea how long we had been at it when Maeryn finally sat down and patted the ground next to her.

Sweat was dripping off me and rolling down my back. I couldn't wait to shower and lay down. "Piper," she said, "have you prayed since he died?" I stared at my hands. "No."

"Then I think that's the final part of our day," she stated. My heart rate picked up, and my palms started to sweat even more.

I didn't know where to start. My hands were clenched, and my throat threatened to tighten up. Suddenly, something broke apart inside me, and I whispered the first real prayer, in all my life.

"Heavenly Father, I need you to know that I desperately need You. I don't know what I'm doing, but I want to do it right and I want to do it for You. Please help guide me through this and give me the wisdom I need to understand what needs to be done. I want to do Your will and not let darkness prevail. Thank you for Your many blessings. Amen." I sighed a huge breath, when suddenly, a shift happened. It was another pressure change. Maeryn looked up at me, her eyes bug eyed.

"You did it. You tipped the scales."

Chapter Twenty-Two

Azrin

I was half a mile from the chapel doing a perimeter check when I felt it– the shift. It cracked through the air like thunder just under the surface– subtle enough that no one else would notice but sharp enough to tear through me like blade.

Piper.

Her emotions spiraled through the tether that bound us. I was so overwhelmed I couldn't distinguish a single feeling, and that terrified me. The old gravel path blurred beneath my feet; every step felt heavier that the last. By the time the chapel came into view, the clouds had thickened, and the wind had picked up. I pushed harder.

Inside, the sanctuary was quiet. I walked in every room and opened every door, searching for her. Finally, I felt her close. I peeked through the crack in the door and I saw Maeryn standing by the windows. She turned when I stepped inside.

"She did it, Azrin. She tipped the scales." Her excitement was palpable, happiness radiating through the room. My chest was heaved –not from running, but from my worry of Piper's well-being.

Everyone gathered in the cafeteria to eat. It wasn't many of us, but enough to make it feel like a little family. Piper sat next to me, looking more relaxed now than I've seen her in years despite the impending war that loomed ahead.

After everyone finished eating, we all helped clean up and do dishes, laughing and cutting up like a family would normally do. After cleaning up, everyone said their goodnights and went their separate ways.

There are many rooms in the chapel, but they've been converted into bedrooms so if anyone needs refuge, they can have privacy. I had changed Piper's wound dressing, and she showered and went to bed.

She left her door cracked and here I am standing here, watching her sleep of the fatigue and anything else she needed reprieve from. There was a softness to her face that I hadn't seen before. She's just incredible.

Eliar found me hours later. "You have changed, my friend. I have no choice but to think it's because of miss Piper." I roll my eyes at him. But I can't deny he's right. I have been alone all of my life. After I fell, I made the choice to live among the people and learn the way they live, love, and work. I've experienced everything but love and it's because I have not been in a position where I felt like I could give myself to someone.

That and the small matter that angels and humans aren't meant to be together, and although I'm fallen, I do hold the hope that one day, I won't be anymore. But every day it gets harder to not succumb to what I am feeling for Piper. To not just tell her how she makes me feel and how I would burn this world down for her.

I just grunted at Eliar and he didn't press any further. He didn't have to. Eliar knows he's right. And I wasn't going to give him the satisfaction of telling him he's right.

I will do anything in my power to make sure Piper finds happiness, but first we have to survive this.

And I will die before I let any harm come to her. She's been hurt under my watch once, but over my dead body will I let that happen again.

Chapter Twenty-Three

I was soaking wet with sweat when Eliar tossed me the wooden staff. I barely caught it in time, the sting in my palms made my teeth clench.

"Again," he said, backing up a few paces and nodding at me to take position. I tried to mimic what he'd shown me, but I still moved like someone unsure of their own strength. Because I was. I didn't know what I was capable of, not really, and definitely not in this aspect.

"You're thinking too much," Eliar said, twirling his own staff with ease. "Just feel it. You already know what do to; I've only told you a thousand times. Just let your body do it."

I gritted my teeth and reset my stance. "I'm not trying to think. I just don't want to screw it up." Eliar gave me a look. "Screwing up is part of learning. The goal isn't to be perfect, it's to be ready." He lunged and I barely got the staff up in time to block. The vibration jarred my arms, but I didn't drop it. That felt like a win.

"You're improving, but barely." Eliar admitted. I shot him a glare. He smirked and went back to his spot to start again. I dropped the staff to my side, muscles burning, sweat clinging to every inch of me like second skin. My heartbeat was finally slowing when the training room door burst open.

It was Maeryn. Her silver hair was wild on her head and her face was flushed like she ran the whole way here. "We've got a problem," she said in between panting. Eliar's body went rigid, and he took a few steps toward her. "What kind of problem?"

"We knew they had been multiplying but it's worse now. They've tripled in the past day from what we understand. We think they may strike tonight. Everywhere."

No one spoke and the weight of her words settled on my shoulders like a bowling ball. Heavy and suffocating. I broke the silence, "Then let's fight." Maeryn nodded in agreement. "You'll need more than a staff."

"I'll get her ready," Eliar said, determination in his voice. I looked down at my blistered hands, the pain in my side is still there, but that seems like such a small problem now. "Then what do we do?"

Maeryn looked at me, her face full of fury, "We survive."

I found him just outside the chapel, sitting on the back steps with his elbows resting on his knees and his head tilted to the sky. The setting sun spilled gold and amber across his face. He didn't look at me right away, but I knew he felt my presence.

"You're limping," Azrin said quietly. I was indeed limping. Between two days of training and my side not being healed, it was crazy that I was able to move at all.

"Yeah, well," I lowered myself down beside him with a wince. "Staff fights are no joke and don't think Eliar knows how to take it easy." That got the faintest twitch at the corner of his mouth. I studied his profile. He looked exhausted. I was worried about him, not only did he bear the pressure of keeping me alive, which I think is an insane request to ask of anybody, but he seemed like he hasn't had happiness in so many years. Seeing him laugh and smile these past couple of days has been great, and I feel like I just watched it all get ripped away from him.

A heavy silence settled between us. "I'm scared," I admitted. "Everything changed so fast, and I finally felt happy and hopeful after meeting you, Eliar, and everyone else with the Remnant. I just wish we had more time." I sighed, choking back the tears that desperately wanted to escape.

"I lost myself when I found my father all those years ago, and now I feel like I have the courage to try and discover who I am, or at least who I want to be. But say we win this war, who am I supposed to be after?"

Azrin locked eyes with me. His were filled with a sorrow that made me want to hug him and promise him it was going to be okay. That I would make sure it would be okay.

"You don't have to know who you'll be," he said. "You just have to decide who you are right now, because right now is what matters the most." I looked down at my scraped hands, then back at him. "But what if who I am right now isn't good enough?"

"Then you fight anyway." His voice getting slightly rougher. "You're not alone, Piper. This weight isn't solely on your shoulders, angel. You may be the one who can end it, or at least push the demons back, but we all shoulder this together."

My throat tightened. He reached over and brushed a piece of hair from my face, his fingers lingering near my cheek.

Then he said, softer than I have ever heard him, "If I could face this all alone, and keep you out of it, and safe, I would do it in a millisecond. But I can't, so just promise me to keep your wits about you and do your best. All this is, is a fight between good and evil. The age-old demons against angels, and although you're so new at this, you've got so much strength and bravery. You only needed training with a sword, but your father made sure he instilled knowledge in you a long time ago."

I leaned into his touch without thinking. "I don't want to lose you," I whispered.

I have never had a boyfriend, and I have never wanted one. But Azrin felt like he was for me. I wanted him to be that for me. I'm determined that this war will be won, and then I can say all the things that I want to say.

His expression changed, but I couldn't make out what he was grappling with. He taught me some nights ago how to close off our emotions to each other, especially during battle so we aren't distracted. Right now, I hated that he closed those off to me.

He placed a kiss on my forehead and then said. "You won't."

Before I could move or respond, the door behind us slammed open. Eliar's voice rang out, "It's time."

Chapter Twenty-Four

The air was still and thick with fog. It was cold outside, but I was sweating. Even with the Remnant footsteps around us and Eliar barking orders at someone behind me, my skin prickled like the fog was hiding something. It felt like the world was holding its breath.

I tightened my grip on the sword Eliar had given me and turned in a slow circle, scanning the shadowed edges of the forest beyond the clearing. I didn't know what I was looking for, but in my training with Maeryn, she taught me what my body was capable of, if I tapped into my full potential. One of those things was that my body could sense something before my brain would be aware. So, I'm testing it out and seeing what I can feel.

Azrin stepped up beside me, his presence bringing me comfort. He looked like he was about to say something when a scream ripped through the air like a blade.

They came out of the trees, shadows with claws. Dozens of them. More than I've ever seen. There was no elegance to the way they moved. It was raw, unfiltered darkness, snarling and ripping toward us with one purpose.

Panic and bile surged up my throat, but I slammed it back down and fell into motion. My job was to help direct the others to where the demons only Azrin, Eliar, and I could see. The pressure settled hard on my shoulders.

Eliar was already shouting commandments. Remnant fighters were springing to life around us, and Azrin was fighting in an instant, his sword flashing as he launched himself into the fray. I took a huge breath and gritted my teeth, squared my shoulders and charged forward.

I ducked beneath a demon's grasp, jamming the end of my sword into its ribs, at least where I thought ribs should be. It let out a distorted shriek and evaporated into black smoke, but two more were already on me. I spun and swung again, heart pounding, and sweat clinging to every part of me. It was absolute chaos.

I moved to try and get a better look to warn the others so they weren't just swinging their weapons blindly, when another one was coming after me. But every time they did,

I moved a little better. I was in mid swing when I heard a voice in my thoughts.

You're doing great. Keep going.

I wanted to look at Azrin and smile and let him know I appreciated his encouragement, but I was scared if I lost focus for even a second, it would be detrimental. I pivoted, swinging hard, catching another demon square in the chest. It shrieked and dissolved into ash before hitting the ground. My muscles burned, but I kept pushing. Another scream pierced the air. Human. A Remnant member had gone down.

I tightened my grip on the sword and pressed forward, weaving between bodies. I saw Azrin fighting not far from me now, cutting through the enemy like a blazing storm. There was something terrifying and beautiful about him in this state. Completely focused, and wholly lethal.

Adrenaline surged in my veins. Sweat blurred my vision. We were holding our ground, just barely. But I'll take it.

The next demon came faster than the others, a blur of shadow and smoke. I barely managed to parry its blow, the force of it jolting through my arms. My grip slipped, but I clenched the sword tighter, refusing to let go. Not when people were counting on me.

"Watch your left!" Eliar's voice rang out.

I pivoted just in time to duck a clawed hand swiping toward my neck. My heart slammed against my ribs as I jabbed the sword into its chest and twisted hard. The demon screeched and disintegrated, but the sound was drowned out by the sheer chaos around me.

They just kept coming.

The smoke thickened with each demon I struck down, like the air itself was choking on darkness. I was doing my best to help others and help myself. I called out directions every chance I could. My arms trembled from exhaustion, my grip on the hilt slick with sweat and blood. I didn't know how much longer I could hold out.

Then, I heard flapping. Huge flapping of bat-like wings. Every head turned skyward, including mine.

Dark-winged figures dropped through the clouds. Their eyes burned with a fury that wasn't human. They hit the ground with enough force to send ripples through the field.

More fallen angels. I don't know why I thought Azrin was the only one, but it never dawned on me that there were others.

They moved fast, coordinated, and terrifyingly graceful. One of them landed directly between me and a demon that had been seconds from reaching me. With a flick of his wrist, he sent it flying through the air like it weighed nothing. His black wings flared, shielding me for a breath before flying back into the fray, his blade lit in the same-ish flame.

I staggered back, stunned, my sword gripped tight. All around us, the tide had turned. The Remnant had been barely holding the line—but now they were fighting alongside people who were once in the army of Heaven itself.

Azrin appeared at my side, blood all over his face and a fire in his eyes. "Reinforcements," he laughed, dark and ruthless. "Some of the fallen still choose to do good."

I stared at him. "Did you call them?"

I just couldn't stop staring at him. The words sounded foreign to me. "Okay," I breathed, looking around at the mess I had found myself in. "You're going to explain that to me later."

Azrin gave me the faintest smirk, ***You got it, but right now we have to win this.*** And with that he placed a quick kiss on my cheek and ran off to help. Will I ever get used to that?

The Hollow Ones were faltering. The tide had shifted. They were more erratic now, almost like they could tell they were losing. I took a deep breath and made my way back to the fight. I swung hard, this time landing a perfect strike across a demon's neck. It shrieked as it vanished into ash.

A shout behind me whirled me around: One of the Remnant had fallen, and another Hollow One was closing in. I moved as fast as I could and slammed my sword into his side just in time. The demon turned on me, and I flinched for half a second. But that was just the time it needed to descend on me. Its claws slashed toward my throat. I closed my eyes waiting for the impact and the pain to surely follow.

When I didn't feel it, I opened my eyes just in time to see Azrin a few feet away, standing over the very demon that attacked me. He sliced the demon through the chest. Smoke exploded outward, curling into nothing.

He turned and closed the distance between us in two strides. He gripped both sides of my face forcing me to look at him. His chest was heaving, anger and worry swirling in his forest green eyes. "Focus, Piper," he growled, not unkindly but scared. His eyes moved back and forth between mine. "You cannot hesitate, because they won't. They will end your life without a second thought."

I nodded, breathless and shaken. Together we ran back into the fray.

My arms are trembling, muscles screaming, and blood – mine and theirs– covered my body. Azrin fights like a storm made flesh, his every move brutal and exact.

Every lesson Maeryn and Eliar drilled into me echoed through my mind. And although I wasn't fighting perfectly, I was fighting with purpose.

The last Hollow One screeched, its form unraveling in a plume of smoke and ash.

The only sounds I could hear were my own fast breathing and quickened heartbeat.

Bodies littered the field. My heart sank. Azrin stood a few feet away, shoulders rising and falling with ragged breath. He turned toward me, covered in black streaks of soot and blood, his eyes locked on mine and before I knew it, my feet were moving. He took me in his arms, fast and with a need. Like he could see I was alive but needed to hold me to truly believe it.

I nodded once, "I'm alive. I'm okay." I could see relief flood through his face. He pulled back a little, his jaw tightened. He didn't say anything, but his eyes were saying everything.

Then Eliar's voice broke the quiet, hoarse and grim. "We need to get everyone out and tend to the wounded. We won this one, but we can't let our guard down." I looked back around the battlefield. The pitch-black night made my stomach roll with queasiness.

I survived my very first battle. This was the closest I've ever come to losing my life. People I just met have died.

My emotions were all over the place and I couldn't settle on just one to focus on. But one thing was crystal clear.

I had no idea what was to come. Nor what I was expected to do. But I was bound and determined to do what I could to end this. To make these new friends of mine, safe. No matter what that looked like.

Chapter Twenty-Five

The battlefield was quiet now, save for the groans of the wounded and the soft crunch of boots over broken ground. I stood in the middle of it, my sword hanging limp in one hand, my other arm trembling from exertion. Smoke curled in the air, mixing with the scent of blood and ash. And a dozen fallen angels were helping everywhere. They were all of massive build like Azrin. Males and females. There were some that wore full body armor and some that didn't even wear a shirt. I noticed that a few had black wings like Azrin's and a few of the shirtless guys had long, angry scars where wings should have been.

One of them passed by me, pausing just long enough to gently guide a wounded member of the Remnant to bench just outside of the chapel.

Azrin stepped up beside me, his chest still rising and falling heavily, but his eyes were on the other angels. "You wanted me to explain how they knew to come here," he said quietly. "All angels, fallen or not, can talk to one another in our thoughts, like you and I can. However, fallen angels can't talk to angels, we're cut off from that." He kept on explaining, "Most of us stay reclused, we don't group together, although some choose to." I looked at him, noting the flicker of emotion that passed through his face—fondness, grief, maybe even guilt.

He looked down at me, "I check in every so often with them. But for the most part, we stay to ourselves. When I reached out tonight, it was like radio silence. I was prepared to lose myself in attempting to win this battle. But seeing this, seeing them... Piper, I can't describe it." He didn't have to. I could feel it. The pride, relief, love, happiness, were all starting to overpower the guilt, fear, and shame he's been carrying around since the day I met him.

A broad-shouldered angel with dark hair, and I kid you not, silver frosted tips, approached us. His presence was calm but commanding.

"Piper, this is Zach," Azrin said nodding toward him. Zach nodded. "Good to finally meet you." His voice was smooth and deep but tinged with exhaustion.

"You're the one that saved Eliar," I said, suddenly remembering the blur of the wings and steel. Zach offered a faint smile.

"That's what a hero does." Azrin laughed, a real belly laugh and I swear it's one of my favorite sounds in the world.

I glanced at his wings. "Why do some of you have wings, and others don't?" I immediately covered my mouth with my hand. There's no way I just met him and asked such a personal question in such a rude way.

I can tell it definitely was a heavy subject by the way his face fell, and before I could apologize, he started explaining. "When we fell," he said slowly, "some of us chose to have another fallen tear them out–out of shame, out of not wanting to be reminded of our failures. Others decide to keep them, for hope of one day achieving redemption." He looked at me and gave a slight smile. "Others do choose to keep them just because they look cool." He gave a tired shrug, "Either way, it's a personal decision."

There was quite a long and uncomfortable silence before I spoke again, "Thank you for coming."

Zach threw his arm over Azrin's shoulder and scuffed up his hair. "I'd follow this guy to the ends of the Earth. Plus, I had to meet the new Veilbreaker. Rumor has it, she's a tough one." He held out his hand for me to shake. When I grabbed it, he said, "Turns out the rumors are true."

* * *

Later, after the wounded had been tended to and dinner had been shared, I found Eliar sitting alone in the garden just outside the chapel. The moonlight stretched across the grass as I approached.

I sat down next to him, and he bumped his shoulder into mine playfully.

"Eliar," I said, soft but certain. "Can you tell me about my father please?"

He took a deep breath and looked up at the sky. "Mark was a good man," he said. "One of the very best. He loved you so much it hurt him. When he learned what you were and what it would cost you, he started searching for a way out. A loophole. Really just anything."

He looked down at his hands before continuing, "The more he learned, the more the weight consumed him. He didn't want this for you. He thought if he could just figure it out first, maybe he could rewrite your story. But the more truth he uncovered, the more it broke him."

Tears pricked my eyes. "He took his own life because of me."

"No," Eliar said firmly. "He took his life because of the darkness pressing in from every side. Because he forgot that this fight isn't ours to bear alone. He just lost sight of who the real enemy was."

I nodded slowly, heart aching but for once things were clearer than they ever have been before. “I won’t make the same mistake.”

He looked at me with something resembling pride in his expression. “No, I don’t think you will.” I stood a little taller, heading back to my room. The weight of my newfound calling still heavy but no longer suffocating.

Chapter Twenty- Six

By morning, I could hardly move. It took everything I had to get myself out of bed, change, and eat. But the sun was up, the sky was a clear blue, and for the first time in days, I felt ready to meet it.

The aftermath of the battle still clung to the earth. Ash and blood still covered the grass and the chapel. To my surprise, the angels were still here. Their tents dotted the grounds behind the chapel, clustered in quiet corners and beneath the old trees. Makeshift beds and weapons leaned against tree trunks.

Some were sitting alone, staring into the distance and others were helping clean up the mess and shoring up the warding lines Maeryn and Eliar had been reinforcing since dawn.

It was strange, watching angels with scarred wings cleaning and stacking crates of medical supplies like field medics. Such mundane things for such magical people.

One of them was laughing quietly with a Remnant member, Kael, over something I didn't catch. They just weren't what I had expected. Not even close.

"Most of them have been out here since before sunrise," Maeryn said beside me, her voice low. "Apparently, they don't sleep much."

"Because they can't?" I asked.

She shrugged, "Or because they don't want to."

Training started not long after that.

The chapel was too crowded, so we moved the fields behind it. Azrin stayed close, but not too close. He was watching me, correcting my form and nodding when I didn't need help. I worked with Eliar on hand-to-hand, with a Remnant soldier named Gideon on stance and reflex, and with one of the angels on blade work- though I was pretty sure he was holding back. They all were.

Regardless, I was holding my own. And for the first time, I actually felt capable. I felt strong and confident. And maybe that was their goal in taking it easy on me. It was working, whatever it was.

I wiped the back of my hand across my forehead, breath catching in short bursts. For October, it shouldn't have been this warm, but all the training had me sweating like it was mid- July. My muscles ached, my shirt clung to my back, and my water bottle suddenly felt like the most precious thing on earth.

I made my way to the edge of the field, where a few folding tables stood with supplies, including more water, which is what I was desperate for. The sun dipped low behind the old chapel, casting long shadows over the grass.

I reach for another bottle, when someone bumps into me from the side. "Oh, man. Sorry, I was not paying attention." I turned, stepping back instinctively.

She was striking. Her golden hair was twisted into a long braid. Her leather jacket literally looked like it was painted on her. What caught my attention the most though, were her black wings, folded tightly behind her. Gah lee, I've never felt just super insecure... but I do now.

"I'm Alex," she said, offering her hand. I took it slowly. "Nice to meet you, I'm Piper." She smiled, a perfect smile, and she handed me the water bottle I was originally reaching for. "I know. Azrin talks about you a lot."

I smiled, unsure of how to respond to that. I wanted to ask if it was good things or bad things but for the intent of not seeming like a crazy human, I opted for a smile. We walked toward the edge of the field, where the trees cast long shadows over the tall grass. Fallen angels were scattered across the clearing. They were training, talking, and helping some of the wounded outside to get some fresh air.

Alex sat beneath a leaning oak and motioned for me to do the same. "He's not like the rest of us, you know," she said after a long moment.

"What do you mean?" I asked, genuinely concerned.

She nodded. "Obviously, we have all fallen from Heaven, for some reason or another. But Azrin, he fell by choice."

I just blinked at her. "Why on earth would he choose that?"

"The last Veilbreaker. He couldn't save him, and in turn it destroyed him." She gave a deep sigh and fiddled with her water bottle. "Nobody blamed him for it, and he was already forgiven. He did everything he could, and he was not at fault." She turned and met my eyes; her expression was filled with sadness. "Azrin couldn't forgive himself."

I nodded. That much I did know, he's told me that himself.

"I think I'm somehow connected to him. He is in my dreams sometimes. Although, it has been a few nights since I've last seen him. He told me about Azrin very vaguely."

She looked at me with confusion, "Have you mentioned this to Azrin?" I nodded.

Some silence stretched between us. After a moment she spoke, "You're stronger than you think, Piper." She stood up and dusted off her clothes. "You may very well be the strongest Veilbreaker I've ever met. Just don't forget that this isn't yours only to carry. We help each other. No matter what."

I smiled at her. I needed that more than she knew. "Do you think Azrin regrets it?" I asked quietly, readjusting my back on the tree.

Alex looked at me for a moment before answering. "I think Azrin regrets everything." Then she looked down at the grass and plucked a few pieces. "Except staying by your side. I think that is the only thing anchoring him right now."

I looked at the chapel. It felt really nice to have someone to talk to. "He's not what I expected."

She laughed. "No one ever is," she gestured around the field, "Especially not the fallen. You'll find most of us are just as messy as humans, if not messier."

Silence passed between us again, but not an uncomfortable one.

"So," she finally said with a smile, nudging me with her shoulder. "You're the Veilbreaker." I gave a soft, and a little sarcastic laugh, "Apparently."

"You don't sound thrilled." She picked up on the sarcasm. I suddenly regretted acting that way because as tough as it's been, I really couldn't imagine having someone else carry this weight on their shoulders.

"I wasn't at first. I was sure there was a mistake because I gave up all of this when my dad died. I just was in a war with my own mind. My dad was a dedicated man of God and for his life to end the way it did and then for my mom to choose her path filled with drugs and alcohol... well let's just say I held anger. A lot of it."

She nodded like she understood. "From what I hear, even though you held that anger and resentment, you still lived a life that wouldn't have indicated that. You may not have attended church or prayed, but you didn't succumb to your inner demons, which is where the Hollow Ones start. They feed on that weakness, on that struggle. You stayed strong, whether you think so or not."

I was fighting back tears. She was right. It would've been so easy for me to get drunk every night, or to live a life that could have led me to a very different place. I made the choice to not cuss, lie, steal, or indulge in what many would call "the finer things in life". I just stayed to myself and unknowingly helped myself resist temptation.

"I needed that. I'm ready to do whatever it takes to end this and to make a difference." I used my jacket sleeve to wipe the tears from my face.

Alex pulled me into a bear hug, "Me too, friend. I have no doubt you will do amazing things. And you can guarantee I will be by your side through it all."

Maeryn's voice called out from the distance. Alex pushed off the tree and offered me a hand. "C'mon, let's see what's going on."

I took her hand and followed her back across the field. And with everything still so uncertain, my heart was at peace.

Chapter Twenty-Seven

The firepit burned low behind us, the last embers of the day crackling like tiny little echoes of what's to come. I stood shoulder to shoulder with Alex and Eliar, cool breeze cutting through the field, the scent of smoke clinging to my skin.

We'd barely finished the evening debrief when Zach strode into the clearing, a folded paper gripped in one scarred hand.

He didn't speak, just handed the paper to Eliar, who opened it with a tension in his jaw I hadn't seen before.

"What is it?" I asked. Eliar scanned the page once, twice, and then passed it to Azrin, who had just joined us. His shoulders tensed the moment his eyes hit the page.

"A Remnant outpost in Calmere," he muttered. "They've gone quiet. The last word from them said the Hollow Ones have doubled in numbers. They need help and fast."

My stomach turned. "How far is that?"

"Three hours north," Eliar said. "But we have to hurry, it could be worse by the time we get there."

"Then we leave now," Azrin said, already walking away to gather his gear.

Alex nodded, "I'll prep the weapons."

Zach tilted his head at me. "You in, Veilbreaker?"

I smiled. It wasn't even a question.

"Oh, I'm in." I said, voice strong and determined. I turned and jogged toward the chapel, adrenaline already kicking in. Inside, the air was warm with heat. It was a nice reprieve on my face. I hadn't realized just how cold I had been.

I threw on a warmer jacket, threw some clothes into a backpack, grabbed my blade, and paused just long enough to tuck a photo of my dad—creased and worn— into my pocket.

Outside, the others were already moving with practiced urgency. Alex passed out weapons like she'd done this a thousand times. Eliar moved through the group, murmuring instructions and quietly checking over armor and gear.

I set my bag on the ground next to me. For there to be so much modern age technology they sure do like to do things in a more old-fashioned way. I don't know why the members of the Remnant from Calmere didn't just call instead of writing. Everyone has a phone, right? Well now that I think about it, I don't even know where mine is. Hopefully, Miriam and Velicity got my messages. Am I going to have a job after this? I have to pay my house payment. Well, this is a fine time to remember this stuff.

Azrin appeared next to me breaking me from my frantic and mundane thoughts. "Hey, angel." I looked up, startled from the sudden tenderness in his voice. "You okay?" he asked, his eyes scanning mine like he could read the chaos behind them

I gave a short laugh. "Define 'okay'. I'm thinking about demons, my job, my mortgage, and now I'm beginning to wonder if the person that made me leave my house is squatting in it."

He chuckled, the sound low and comforting. "I can help ease your mind for a few of those things. No to the squatter, once I made sure you were safe, I went back to check things out. I even locked your door when I left. Your job is fine, Miriam is a member of the Remnant and has been a big help in keeping tabs on you." He smiled, (and good grief he's a gorgeous man.) "We can take care of your mortgage after we return. So just focus on the demons for now. That is the most pressing."

My expression must have changed because he turned until he stood right in front of me. He reached out and brushed a hair behind my ear and rested his hand on the side of my face. "You're scared. Everyone is. But we are going together. Never forget that you're not alone."

I nodded. "You really think we can do this?"

He tilted his head, he almost looked confused that I would ask him such a question. "Of course I do. And if for some reason we don't, Piper. I want you to know that I have your back. Not because of my promise, but because I believe in you. I am so proud of you."

I blinked hard, forcing down the lump rising in my throat. His words settled into something deep within me. They sank into cracks I hadn't realized were still wide open.

"Thank you," I managed, my voice barely above a whisper. Azrin didn't answer, he just looked at me like he was contemplating something, but what, I had no idea.

I thought I saw him lean closer ever so slightly, when Eliar's voice rang out. "Time to move!"

Boots scuffed against the gravel driveway. Azrin pulled his hand away reluctantly, like he didn't want to. He stooped down and picked up my bag for me, I took it from him and looked around. Tension hummed beneath the surface of everyone, Alex's masked only by her cracking knuckles and mumblings of something about how she hopes the Hollow Ones haven't gotten any uglier.

We piled into a black SUV. I somehow ended up in the back seat between Azrin and Zach, while Eliar is in the driver seat and Alex in the passenger seat.

The engine roared to life, and we pulled away from the chapel. I turned to look back once. Everybody was standing around waving us goodbye and giving us encouragement. From what I understood the other fallen angels were going to come assist us after we arrived. Apparently, flying is faster than driving. Who knew?

I faced forward again, gripping the edge of my seat until my knuckles ached.

My stomach was in knots when we pulled onto the road. But at least I had three hours to convince myself that I am going to do well and that my training had paid off.

I say a silent prayer, asking for guidance and protection into this battle I'm heading straight into, like stepping into a fire and trusting I won't burn.

Chapter Twenty-Eight

I must've dozed off at some point, because when the truck finally slowed to a halt, I jerked awake like I had been awoken by a nightmare.

Eliar turned and looked at me, his face serious and hard. "You need to look through your Veilbreaker eyes. Otherwise, you will not be able to see the way you need to." I blinked the sleep from my eyes and nodded, my heart already racing. My fingertips tingled, the way they always did when something unseen crept just beneath the surface of the world. I took a slow breath and focused like Maeryn taught me, letting the veil between, seen and unseen, slide back like a curtain.

And there it was. Black tendrils clung to buildings like rot, stretching down alleys and across the pavement. The only way I know how to describe it, was like an alternate universe. It's what's happening behind the scenes that humans, (crazy I have to use that word now) can't see. Or who at least who aren't willing and actively searching from what I've learned from my studies with Maeryn. Which I am now assuming is how Eliar and some of the Remnant can see.

Azrin was already out of the vehicle, sword in hand, scanning the area like he could feel it too. Every heartbeat, every rustle of wings, every whisper of demonic movement skittering along the shadows of the ruined city- it all collided into one roaring current inside me.

I tightened my grip on the blade by my side. Calmere was a ghost town. Windows shattered. Doors hanging from hinges. Azrin turned and looked at the group. "Stay alert. We don't know what's waiting for us."

Zach followed, then Alex, who muttered, "They weren't exaggerating," as she scanned the wreckage. Her wings twitched, half-flared like a shield.

Eliar's jaw was tight. "We find whoever's left and regroup fast. If the Hollow Ones are still here, then they will see us before we see them."

My stomach twisted as my boots crunched over broken glass and more ash. This place felt like a graveyard. We moved in a formation, cautious, weapons at the ready. Every gust of wind felt like fingers crawling up my spine.

"Over here!" a voice rasped out, low and desperate. A man stumbled out from behind a crumbled stone wall, blood streaked down his face and one arm hanging limp at his side. He had a tattoo on his neck, of the Remnant symbol. "They came through two nights ago," he choked out. "They tore through everything. We tried to hold them back. We tried so hard but they just kept-"

Azrin caught him as he swayed, steadying him gently. "How many are left?"

The man coughed. "Eight? Maybe ten. They're all scattered and hiding."

My throat tightened, but I forced myself to swallow the fear that threatened to consume me. There would be time to feel later. Right now, we have a job to finish.

I looked up and met Azrin's eyes. He gave me a nod, giving me reassurance that we're okay. We moved fast after that. The team split in two. Eliar and Zach went one way around the perimeter in search for survivors, while Azrin, Alex, and I made our way deeper into the ruined city, the scent of ash and sulfur curling around every corner.

I drew in a deep breath, trying to steady my thoughts and emotions so they didn't overwhelm or distract Azrin. Before I knew it three demons came out of nowhere, lunging from the dark shadows where they had been waiting.

Azrin moved instantly, his sword flashed silver, catching the first demon in midair and throwing it backward with a thunderous crack. Alex met the second with a roar, her wings unfurling all the way as she slammed it into a crumbling wall.

The third was already on me, I sidestepped, dodging its claws, and slammed my blade into its chest. The demon shrieked as it turned into ash, the sound rattling deep in my bones.

I barely had time to recover before Alex grabbed my arm. "You okay?" I nodded, though my heart was thudding so loud it was all I could hear.

Azrin was already scanning the alley again, jaw clenched, his eyes colder than I've ever seen them. The veil was super thin here, so I didn't have to focus too hard, if at all, to see what the angels were seeing. A sharp whistle echoed above, followed by the sound of wings. I looked up just in time to see three more fallen angels descend from above, their dark wings stretching wide as they landed hard around us. My heart lightened at the sight of the familiar faces.

"We got here as soon as we could." One of them called out. Azrin only nodded, but I could feel the shift in his stance. He closed his emotions off to me so I could focus but I could almost feel the relief emanating off of him.

We pressed deeper into the city, searching the ruined buildings and alleyways. In the basement of a church, we found five more survivors, huddled behind broken pews and barricades of overturned furniture. Their eyes lit with cautious hope when they saw us.

Something grabbed me from behind. I barely had time to scream before its claws dug into my shoulder and yanked me off of my feet. The world blurred, spinning fast as I hit the ground hard. I kicked and fought, but the demon was massive. Twice the size of any I'd seen thus far.

Azrin's roar split the air. He was absolute wrath. His wings flared wide and his eyes lit with a fire I'd never seen before. The demon didn't stand a chance. In seconds, it was ash.

Azrin dropped to his knees beside me, his hands shaking as he reached for my face. "Piper-Piper. Look at me; you're okay."

The pain was absolutely excruciating. I could feel it throughout my whole arm and even up my neck. "I'm fine," I whispered, even though my voice was trembling, and I was starting to see black spots. I had barely gotten back on my feet when another scream tore through the air. I flinched, but it jolted something inside me. It snapped me out of the haze of blood loss and brought me back from the edge of passing out. My shirt was soaked with my blood, my arm felt like it had been set on fire, but I pushed forward anyways.

I turned toward the sound, pain flaring with every step, but I didn't stop. "Piper!" Azrin's voice sliced through the chaos. "You're hurt- stop!"

I spun toward him, my chest heaving "There's no time! Let's go!" He didn't argue. He clenched his jaw and fell in step beside me. We rounded the corner, and the Hollow Ones were flooding in from the far end of the street, dozens of them.

I gritted my teeth, gripped my blade, and ran into the mayhem. Every movement sent sheer pain through my body, but I pushed forward anyway. I was fighting for the people who couldn't help themselves.

Something sharp raked across my back. I stumbled and dropped to my knees. The world tilted sideways, and my ears started ringing.

I could barely hear a voice shout my name loud and desperate. Azrin. I blinked through the blur just in time to see him cut through two demons like they were paper. Then he saw me- really saw me- and whatever was left of his restraint burned away.

His wings flared and his hands ignited with blue fire. He was no longer fighting like he was on a mission. He was fighting like he was about to lose something he couldn't bear to live without. Every Hollow One between us disintegrated under his fury. I could feel the heat from where I was still on the ground.

He reached me just before I collapsed, his arms catching me, dragging me to his chest. "You stubborn, impossible woman." He breathed, his voice shaking. "I told you that you were hurt and needed to stay back."

I smiled weakly my eye lids fluttering. "I wouldn't be me if I listened to you. Or if I didn't do what I could to help." He placed his forehead against mine.

Through my peripheral, I could see my new friends fighting like their lives depended on it. The world went black before I could hear what Azrin said back.

Chapter Twenty-Nine

Azrin

"Piper." Her name was a ragged sound on my lips. She didn't answer. Her body was limp in my arms, her blood warm and slick beneath my hands. My mind blanked and everything else disappeared. All I could see was her.

"No," I whispered. "No, no, no-" I dropped to my knees with her, holding her like my world would stop if I didn't. "Stay with me," I begged. "You're not done yet. We need you still. I need you."

Eliar was suddenly there beside us, his breath ragged. "We have to move her- now." I shook my head, "I can't.. I can't let her go."

"You have to!" He snapped, already assessing her wounds. "There is absolutely no time to waste. She may be the Veilbreaker but she is still human, Azrin."

I didn't want to. God help me I did not want to let her out of my arms. But I forced myself to my feet and I laid her gently on a collapsed slab of stone, trying my best to keep her out of dirt and debris. I hovered while Eliar worked, muttering words and rummaging through a makeshift kit pulled from his bag.

I stood there, useless, my hands covered in her blood and my chest cracking open like something sacred had just been ripped out of me.

A cry from deeper in the city cut through my thoughts. Alex was surrounded. Zach's wing had been torn. The others were holding the line, but just barely.

I looked back at Piper. Her skin was so pale. The only reassurance I had was that I could still feel her through our bond. It was weak, but it was there.

I stood. I would not let this be for nothing.

I left Eliar with her, my heart splintering with every step, and I tore back into the fray. My anger carried me. My love for her sharpened into something lethal. Every demon that got near my blade was ash within seconds. I lost track of everything.

I didn't care about pain or burn out. I only cared about getting back to her, about making sure the world she woke up to was still standing. I pushed hard, which made the others push harder.

One by one, the demons began to fall. We found more survivors. Some of the fallen who could still fly carried the critically wounded back to Maeryn, their wings blades of shadow cutting through the gloom.

Still, she didn't wake. But I could still feel her. The fragile thread between us- the bond I swore I wouldn't ever need- it pulled tight in my chest, humming with a quiet fight. She was still here, and she was still fighting.

That was enough to keep me moving. Eventually, the city quieted, and the battle was over. We'd won, but not without scars.

I couldn't wait any longer; I gathered Piper into my arms as carefully as I could and took to the skies.

The wind roared past as I flew, but I kept my grip on her steady. Her head rested against my shoulder. She was warm, but she was still unconscious. I flew higher, away from the smoke and destruction.

I had been flying for what felt like an eternity when I felt a flutter. The faintest movement. Her hand curled ever so slightly against my chest.

"Piper?" My voice broke around her name. She stirred again. I felt her soul before I saw her eyes- flickering through our bond like flame refusing to be snuffed out. A breath escaped her lips, her eyelids fluttered, eyelashes brushing against my collarbone.

"....Azrin?"

I exhaled like I hadn't been breathing the whole time. "You're okay, angel." I pressed my forehead gently to hers, letting my voice fall into the space between us. "You're safe."

She blinked up at me, still in a daze. "What happened?" I gave her a soft smile. "I tried to tell you that you were too hurt to help, and you tried to prove me wrong, which resulted in proving me right anyways."

Her lips twitched like she was fighting a smile. "Yeah, sounds like me." I wanted to laugh and smile like a lunatic, but the tightness in my chest hadn't eased up yet. "You shouldn't have done that, angel," I whispered. "You scared me to death."

"You're a fallen angel, I didn't think anything scared you." She murmured, her eyes trying to stay open. I huffed a breath of laughter, but she had no clue how wrong she was. I didn't' used to fear much, but I didn't have anything to lose. Now I have her, and I have everything to lose.

She shifted weakly, her hand brushing over the fabric at my chest. "You didn't leave me."

My heart filled with sorrow. This woman knew so much heart ache and abandonment that it made me physically sick. "I never will. Your days of being alone are completely and irrevocably over."

Silence fell between us. She tucked her head beneath my chin. "I knew you'd save me. You always do."

I would always save her. Not just on the battlefield but in whatever aspects she needs. Always. She had no idea the lengths I would go to for her. I would watch the world we are so desperately trying to save burn for her if she simply asked me to.

As the chapel finally came into view, lights glowing faintly like beacons in the dark, I tightened my grip on her. "You're going to rest," I told her. "They're going to stitch you up better than Eliar's rushed patch job and then I need you to rest. And then we will figure out what's next."

She placed a kiss on my cheek. It felt like electricity burned through my entire body. "You're bossy when you're worried," she mumbled. I didn't even argue, because I was. I was incredibly terrified.

And for the first time, I couldn't imagine a world without her in it. I didn't *want* to imagine a world without her. There is no me without her. I hugged her closer to me, enjoying our last moments together alone before the swarm that would form upon our arrival.

Chapter Thirty

Azrin

The room was quiet- save for the sound of her breathing. It was steady, thankfully. She hadn't stirred since I laid her down several hours ago. I sat beside her, my elbows on my knees, just waiting.

I watched her like someone might take her if I so much as dared to blink. She looked smaller somehow, tucked beneath the blankets. Fragile in a way she would never let herself be when conscious.

Bruises bloomed beneath her skin at her temple, angry and dark. Blood had crusted at her hairline. It had been cleaned up some but there was still a little there. I hated seeing her like this.

I exhaled through my nose, my jaw tightening. The fire I'd used in that battle had nearly consumed me. That rage hadn't come from vengeance. It had come from fear. Not fear of death, or of losing the fight. But of losing her.

I had no idea I could still fear something that much. I didn't know that I could *love* someone so much that it could lead to my undoing.

I sat back, forcing myself to lean into the chair. My eyes drifted to her hand– resting on top of the blanket. I reached out for it and then paused. Then I left my fingers brush hers. Just enough to feel the heat of her skin.

A quiet knock pulled my head up. Eliar entered with a damp cloth and another cup of water. He paused at the sight of me still there. "You need rest," he said gently. I didn't answer and he didn't press.

He walked over to the side of the bed and started carefully checking her bandages. "She's strong, you know." I nodded, of course I knew that. "Yeah, I know." He looked at me for a long moment. "You almost burned out, Azrin." He just wants to state the obvious, that much is apparent.

I just nodded again. "I did." Eliar's brow furrowed, but he only nodded. "She seems to ground you." This man cannot read a room. I looked at him, "She destroys me."

And somehow, that's what I needed. The woman with fire in her eyes and pain in her past. The one who still found a way to hope even when everything had been stripped from her.

I leaned forward, brushing a loose strand of hair from her cheek with trembling fingers. "Come back to me, angel." I whispered. "Please."

Our bond stirred faintly, causing warmth to bloom low in my chest. I stood up and walked over to Eliar. "She's fighting. But how much longer until she wakes up?" He nodded. "She's not done yet. Just go take a walk or something and clear your head some. It will do you some good."

Then he left me alone, closing the door behind him. The sun dipped lower in the sky. Shadows had started crawling up the walls. And I stayed right here, watching her breathe. Memorizing every inch of her face. Her freckles, the little scar on her chin, and the way her lips parted when she dreamed. I didn't deserve her. I'd never claim that.

But I would die to protect her. And I would live to make sure she never had to do anything alone again.

Chapter Thirty-One

Waking up felt strange. It felt like my bones were made of cement and someone had laid a weight on my chest. My throat was dry, and my head ached. My ribs throbbed with every breath. But I was alive. That realization struck first. The second was that I was in my bed. The third was that I wasn't alone.

The gentle light spilling from the window illuminated him perfectly.

Azrin was slumped in the chair beside my bed. His elbows were resting on his knees, his fingers threaded through his hair. He looked like he hadn't moved in days. I swallowed, the sound raspy and loud.

"You look like crap."

His head snapped up.

And then-God help me- he smiled. He jumped out of the chair and rushed to kneel beside the bed. "You're awake," he breathed, his voice quiet and excited. His hand hovered at his sides like he wasn't sure where he was allowed to go.

"You almost died, angel," he said. His eyes were full of sorrow, but his emotions were mixed with relief, guilt, happiness, and love? Is that right? "I remember." My voice broke. "Is everyone okay? Did we win?"

"We did win. I guess we have you to thank for that really. After you got hurt the second time, it was...motivation to get everyone out of there before things got any worse. Although, I'm not sure how that is possible, you getting hurt is the worst thing in my book." His restraint appeared to have lost, he reached up and placed his hand on the side of my face, gently.

"You didn't think twice before running back into battle even after I told you that you were already hurt." His voice wavered a tad, like he was holding back tears.

I met his soft green eyes. "Because I couldn't think. And I didn't need to think. They needed our help, so I went to help." He stared at me. I leaned into his touch. "I'd do it again," I said softly. "Every time. Especially for innocent people, the fallen, Eliar, and *you*."

Azrin closed his eyes for a beat like the words physically hit him. When they opened again, there was a storm behind them. Grief, rage, and devotion were swirling around. "I don't deserve that kind of loyalty," he whispered.

"Maybe not," I said, giving him the best smile I could muster. "But you have it anyway."

He brushed his fingers against my temple, it was sore, which is weird because I don't remember hitting my head. The calluses on his fingers were rough but his touch was impossibly gentle.

"You were out for two days," he said. "We got you back and Eliar and Maeryn stitched you up. Everyone has been worried about you."

I took a deep breath, his touch giving me goosebumps. "I'm sorry."

He chuckled. "Don't be, just don't do that again." He pressed his forehead to mine, which seems to have turned into our thing. I closed my eyes and whispered, "I can't make that promise." He nodded, "I didn't think you could, but it was worth a shot."

We stayed like that for a moment. I pulled back just a little and looked at him. Really looked at him. He had dark circles under his eyes and dried blood still on his clothes. He looked absolutely exhausted. "You didn't leave me," I whispered.

He didn't answer. He didn't need to. Because I knew. I felt it.

Whatever this was between us, it wasn't just the promise he made anymore. It was choice. And he kept choosing me. Every time.

Chapter Thirty-Two

The quiet and sweet moment was abruptly interrupted when a sudden and heavy urge took over. Good grief, all the liquid had built up and was currently wreaking havoc on my kidneys. I sat up too fast and the world spun, my ribs shrieked, and my body quickly reminded me that it was still recovering. I threw the covers off. "I have got to use the bathroom. Immediately. Like right this second."

He blinked at me and busted out laughing. He helped me stand and walked with me, holding me up. "Two days unconscious. I'm honestly surprised you didn't wet the bed." He muttered through his laughter as he steadied me with an arm around my waist.

I couldn't even come up with a witty comeback, all of my focus was on not wetting myself. With his help, I limped my way down the hallway. But we finally made it.

Once that glorious moment of relief passed and we returned to my room, I plopped, not so gracefully, onto the edge of my bed and took inventory. I had bruises everywhere, I was definitely sore and absolutely starving, but despite these things, I was alive. And oddly enough, eager to get back into training and helping where I can.

"What's that look for?" Azrin asked.

I shrugged my shoulders. "I'm just ready."

He tilted his head and crossed his arms as he leaned against the windowsill. "Okay, sure. Ready for what?"

I took a deep breath, and my back twinged in pain. "Whatever comes next. Planning or fighting. Just fixing all of this. I'm ready to get back at it."

Azrin raised an eyebrow. "You do realize that you were nearly dead forty-eight hours ago."

I shot him a playful look. "And now I'm not. Look, I don't know how to describe it, but I'm excited even though I have faced death at least three times now." He didn't respond right away. He just looked at me with that unreadable expression of his. Then finally, he nodded.

"Alright, angel. Let's get you fed first. Then we'll go wreak havoc."

I grinned. "Now you're speaking my language."

Azrin offered his hand without a word. I hesitated, mostly out of pride, but the second I stood up on my own, a sharp jolt of pain shot through my side and stole the air from my lungs.

"Yep," I muttered, grabbing his arm. "Still very much in pain." He slipped an arm around my waist, steady and careful, and I leaned into him more than my pride wanted to admit. Each step sent dull aches rippling through my ribs and back, but his grip was strong and solid.

"Let me know if it's too much," he said, his voice low.

"If I let you carry me, I don't think Zach and Alex will ever let me live it down."

He smirked. "Fair enough. But I'll do it if I have to."

The walk to the dining area felt longer that it usually does. I hated how slow I was and how weak I felt. But Azrin never rushed me. He matched my pace like he had nowhere else in the world he'd rather be.

When we finally made it to the small cafeteria, my stomach let out a monstrous growl. Azrin looked down at me, smiled and raised and eyebrow. "I take it you're ready to eat."

I didn't even have the energy to be embarrassed that my body did that. "Starving," I admitted.

He helped me ease into the seat first before grabbing us both a plate. I used the time to catch my breath, pushing past the stubborn ache in my ribs. By the time he returned, my stomach was eating my back, or at least that's how it felt.

Azrin set the plate down in front of me, sliding into the seat across the table. "Eat up, angel."

I paused mid-bite. "Can I ask you a question?"

He raised a brow, feigning innocence. "You can ask me anything you want."

I took a deep breath, suddenly nervous for whatever reason. "You always call me that," I said softly, "Angel."

He leaned closer to me and crossed his arms on the table. His gaze unreadable, but I could feel a slight lurch in his emotions, almost like a hint of panic. "Do you want me to stop?" he asked, his voice low and slow.

"No," I said too quickly. "I was just wondering...why?" I could feel an immediate sense of relief from him, the panic gone. I fought a smile when I realized that he was worried that I didn't like his nickname for me, which meant he cares what I think, and for some reason that meant everything to me.

Azrin turned fully toward me, his piercing green eyes looking deep into mine. This must be what people mean when they say that time stands still. When he looks at me this way, it really does feel like everything stops except for us.

"Because you are," he said simply. "Not in the same way, obviously, but because to me you are an angel. You showed up in while I was deep, many years deep, in brooding, in feeling sorry for myself. You reminded me what light and happiness looks like, despite what's happening around me, I can still choose to find happiness. You reminded me what I'm fighting for, what I'm choosing happiness for."

The lump in my throat seemed to grow larger with every word he said.

"I was lost long before this war, Piper. But then there was you, and sure at first it was an obligation, but now, it's a want. No, not everything got fixed for me over night, but you reminded me that hope is a good thing. You helped me remember that I have a purpose."

I blinked fast, suddenly too warm, and too full of feelings I wasn't ready to name. "Azrin," I whispered but my voice caught, and I wasn't able to say anything else.

His hand found mine under the table, fingers brushing slowly before settling between mine. "I call you angel," he said, "because to me you are one. And at the risk of sounding too possessive, you are *my* angel." He reached up and brushed my hair behind my ear, never breaking eye contact.

Warmth bloomed in my chest, slow and steady like the first light of dawn. I tried to fight the pink rising in my cheeks, but to no avail. I couldn't even say anything, I just looked down at my food and started stabbing at it.

Azrin chuckled, low and satisfied. He could feel my embarrassment through the bond, and I didn't even care that he knew what he was doing to me.

Chapter Thirty-Three

Azrin steadied me as we stepped into the sun, his hand warm at my back, ready to catch me if I collapsed. Which I would never let myself do. Especially in front of this man. I hated needing help- but after this near dying experience, I wasn't about to argue with his over-protectiveness. Besides, if I tore a stitch Eliar would never let me hear the end of it.

We crossed the threshold of the chapel, and the sound of clashing swords and shouted commands met us. The yard had been turned into a bigger makeshift training field. Sunlight filtered through the trees, making this moment feel as if the world itself was holding its breath.

Zach spotted us first. He paused mid-spar, his wings half-flared behind him. One was wrapped in a thick bandage, but his grin was bright and full of life. "Well look who decided to rejoin the living."

Alex turned at his voice. Her blonde hair was braided back, arm in a sling, but her eyes lit up when they landed on me. "Piper!" She jogged over, careful not to jostle her arm. "You scared us to death."

I smiled. I loved my friends. "You're one to talk! You and Zach took on a whole horde by yourselves!"

"Someone had to," she said, nudging my uninjured side. Others gathered too. Familiar faces, and the people that we were able to rescue. Their wounds were healing, and they seemed happy despite recent events. A few of them waved from the shaded edges of the tree line.

"You're really okay?" Zach asked, his expression more serious now.

I nodded, "I'm okay. Just sore, but ready to get back into kicking your butt in training and discussing what to do next."

Azrin shifted beside me, his gaze sharp as ever, but I could feel the tension easing in him. "What happened after I went down?" I asked.

Zach exhaled slowly, exchanging a glance with Alex. "The Hollow Ones got stronger, and it happened so fast. They were feeding off the fear, the despair, the anger in that city. People are hanging on by threads, Piper. The cost of things is too high, and people are struggling to make ends meet. Depressions is rising, drug abuse is also on the rise and it's all cracking the door wide open and making easy targets for the demons."

"Humans are trying to become numb, so they don't feel anything. They have lost all sense of hope. And that's what the demons thrive on the most."

A chill ran through me despite the warmth of the sun. I swallowed hard. "So, we are fighting more than just demons."

"We're fighting hopelessness," Azrin said. "And it's everywhere." The silence that followed settled heavy over the group. But then I looked around again– at the training, at the laughter, at everyone healing together. We were still here, still choosing to fight even when that seems like the harder option.

"We just need to regroup. We cannot afford to get down on ourselves and lose sight of what we are doing this for. We have to close the veil. I realize it's only a temporary solution but maybe it will be a step in the right direction too. As long as people feel content living in sorrow, which is what it seems like the demons do. Then they're not going to have a reason to look for hope." I looked at each of them individually. "Getting rid of the demons will be the first step into giving people their hope back."

For a moment, no one said anything. The only sounds were the wind rustling through the trees and the birds chirping.

Eliar cleared his throat and gave a small nod. I hadn't even noticed he walked up. "Hope is a hard thing to hold onto when the world keeps trying to crush it. But you're right, if we take away the source of darkness, maybe people will finally be able to breathe again. Maybe they'll remember how to live."

Zach rubbed at his shoulder, wincing slightly but nodding too. "We can start small." One block, one neighborhood, one city at a time. That'll give humans a little room to breathe and hopefully find their footing sooner rather than later."

Alex adjusted the sling on her arm, her voice full of determination. "We can't save everyone, and we can't be everywhere, but we can't sit back either."

I glanced at Azrin beside me. He hadn't said anything, but I could feel him. That tether between us hummed, alive and steady, comforting me in more ways than I could ever convey in words.

"We'll regroup tonight," Eliar said, stepping forward. "Plans, Shifts. Assignments. We are just going to do what we can with what we've got."

Everyone nodded and dispersed. A little boy ran by past me, chasing a butterfly, his happiness beaming through the air like a ray of sunlight. It hit me right then–this is what we were fighting for. Not just survival, But for joy, laughter, and a future full of hope and faith.

Azrin nudged my elbow. "You ready for what's next, angel?"

I turned toward him, a half- smile forming despite the ache in my body. "I was born for it."

Something in his expression softened. "Then lead the way, Veilbreaker."

Chapter Thirty- Four

Azrin

The morning air was thick with fog and dew. I stood near the edge of the field, just past some fellow angel's tents. My eyes followed across the clearing–her movements slower than usual since she's still healing, but she's more determined than ever. Every time she stumbled, she pushed forward. Every time someone offered help, she waved it off with that same fire in her eyes.

She didn't realize it yet but she's already changing everything. "

You always watch her like that?" Zach's voice cut through my thoughts. I glanced sideways. He approached quietly, one arm still in a sling, dark hair wind-tossed and wild.

"I don't mean to," I said. "It just happens."

Zach stopped beside me, following my gaze. "She's something, huh?"

"She's more than that," I said quietly. "She's everything." He didn't say anything at first. Just nodded slowly, his expression unreadable.

Zach's gaze lingered on Piper for another moment, making me highly irritable. He spoke again, his voice quieter this time. "She knows about your promise, doesn't she?"

I nodded once, my jaw tight. "Yeah, I told her everything."

"And?"

"She took it better than I anticipated. I always underestimate her and what she's capable of."

A beat passed. Then he shifted slightly, fixing me with a look that didn't feel casual anymore. "You need to tell her the rest, Az."

I glanced at him. "The rest?"

He raised an eyebrow. "Don't play dumb. You think no one notices the way you look at her? The way you fall apart every time she's hurt? You'd burn the world for the girl, and we all know it. But does she?"

I didn't answer. Mostly because I didn't know how.

Zach pressed, his tone still calm but firm. "You made a promise to her dad. Fine. Noble, even. But what you're doing now...this is different. You're not protecting her out of duty anymore, Azrin. You're doing it because *you love her.*"

I stared at the ground, clenching my fists at my sides. "She's been through enough. The last thing she needs is to carry me on top of everything else."

"She doesn't need to carry you," Zach said. "She just needs to know. And maybe, just maybe, she deserves to know that someone loves her enough to fight hell itself just to keep her breathing."

I looked up again, to where she stood in the sun; she was beautiful. She was bruised but unshaken, her hair was messy, but she looked just as good to me. My voice was low when I finally answered. "I don't know how. I've never done this."

Zach clapped his hand on my shoulder. "You'd better figure it out. If anyone deserves something real–It's Piper."

Chapter Thirty-Five

By late afternoon, the camp had taken on an oddly comforting kind of rhythm—the wounded getting their bandages changed, fallen angels training, and Remnant members hanging up clean clothes to dry. I'd spent the better part of the day walking and doing stretches with Alex, doing my best not to tear my stitches open. Every time I winced, someone gave me a look like they might just physically glue me to a bed. I was already over it. I needed to be useful.

By the time the sun dipped toward the horizon, casting a golden haze over the chapel grounds, I was sitting on the back steps with a cup of lukewarm tea, my ribs and back thanking me for giving them reprieve. The door creaked behind me, causing me to jump.

"I thought I'd find you out here," Azrin said quietly, sitting beside me with a grace that I'd give anything to have. He handed me a clean cloth. "You're bleeding through your bandage again."

I sighed and peeled back the edge of my shirt. Sure enough, a fresh stain was forming. "Oh, it's fine. I barely even feel it anymore." Azrin just raised an eyebrow. Duh, he can feel my pain. "Okay," I admitted, "it hurts ever so slightly."

He worked on changing my bandage in silence, cleaning the wound with a practiced care. His touch was gentle, but the quiet between seemed to hold more weight than usual.

"What's on your mind?" I asked.

He glanced up at me, then back at my injury. "Nothing really. Zach and I had a talk and it's just on my mind."

I waited but he didn't elaborate. He stayed quiet for a while and it felt like he was really debating against his own self, so I didn't press.

Finally, he spoke. "He seems to think that I need to have a conversation with you about something. And I can't even believe I'm even taking his advice." I could feel his emotions. They were everywhere. He pulled my shirt down and slowly turned me to face him.

"Okay, have a conversation about what?"

A pit formed in my stomach. Azrin just looked at me. It was the kind of look that made it hard to breathe. The kind that you see in movies or read about in books and wish that one day you would have someone to look at you like that.

"Look, I know I made a promise to your father. But I need you to know that I don't just want to protect you. You've changed everything. The way I see the world. The way I see myself. You helped me find something I thought I'd lost a long time ago...hope. Not just in this war, but in everything right now and for whatever comes after."

I blinked, stunned into silence, but he continued. "And I know we are standing on the edge of something dark and terrible," he added, his voice low, "but I need you to know that I would face this a thousand times if it meant I'm doing it with you."

"Azrin.."

He shook his head slightly, like he wasn't expecting me to say anything back. But I reached for his hand, lacing our fingers together. He exhaled slowly, as if after everything, he was finally letting himself breathe.

We sat in stillness, hands intertwined, the fading sun painting everything gold. His emotions were all over the place still, but I could mostly make out the loudest one—relief. A kind of quiet, comforting relief that settled over him like he hadn't let himself relax until now. He had hope. Like maybe, just maybe, he could finally want something without feeling guilty.

I squeezed his hand. "You're not alone, anymore." I said softly. He didn't say anything, just shifted slightly so our shoulders touched. It wasn't much, but it felt like everything. Like we knew the weight of the world was still there, but we knew we were facing it together.

The sun dipped lower, casting long shadows across the floor. And I let the warmth of the moment settle in my chest.

Despite the impending war we were facing, I was happy. And for now, that was a win.

Chapter Thirty-Six

It was strange to me how easy a person could find a routine in such a difficult time. In the month since the rescue mission, the chapel had become more than a sanctuary- it had become a base, a training camp, and a home. Some more fallen angels had come to help and there were more tents put up, and it was oddly cozy.

Eliar's system of patrols and assignments kept everyone busy and alive. Every day, we took turns going into the towns overrun with Hollow Ones, pushing them back, trying to get the humans some reprieve to think clearly and find their hope.

Training filled the hours on the days I wasn't out on patrol. I didn't think my muscles could get anymore sore, but each day proved to me that they in fact, can. Bruises were also fairly consistent as well, but so was the laughter and teasing. The loyalty bled deeper than anything I'd ever known.

We were a family. A strange, half winged, battle-scarred family but they were mine all the same.

Zach was like the brother I never had. He was protective and loudmouthed, and he was always trying to one-up Alex in training drills. He really was the life of the place. He was really full of himself now that his wing was healed.

Alex, with her sling now gone and her sass back in full force, had taken upon herself to toughen me up emotionally and physically. I didn't mind though. I needed it for what we were to face in the future.

The sun hung low overhead, casting long dappled shadows across the clearing as Alex and I squared off once again. Her blonde braid whipped behind her like a ribbon of defiance. Her movements were precise, and it was good to see her feeling better.

"Again," she said, her breath short. "You're starting to get lazy."

I grunted, swinging the practice staff with more force than grace. "I'm not lazy. I'm just sore and exhausted."

Alex smirked. "Well good. Then we're doing something right."

We circled each other in the packed dirt, sweat soaking through my shirt and stinging my eyes. But there was no complaining from me. Not after I all but demanded that everyone stop going easy on me. If the enemy wasn't going to pull punches, then neither should they.

Every jab, every parry, every hit reminded me of the task I had at hand and important it was that I be as prepared as I could possibly be. By the time Alex finally called it, I was doubled over, hands on my knees, and my lungs dragging in air.

"Hey, you did good," she said, brushing a stray hair from her flushed face. "You improve every single day."

I straightened up, swiping sweat from my forehead with my sleeve. "I think you knocked out a kidney."

She snorted and clapped me on the back. "That's the spirit."

We parted ways with a wave, and I made a slow, achy trek to the shower. I peeled off my clothes as easily as I could without upsetting my bones even more. I stood under the spray of the water for longer than necessary, just letting the water carry away the dirt, sweat, and soreness.

By the time I dressed and made my way to the makeshift dining area, I found it had been moved outside to accommodate the growing crowd. The sky was shifting into soft golds and pinks. Laughter echoed around the campfires which made my heart swell. I used to think I preferred being alone, that it was better that way, but I honestly don't know how I could ever go back.

The smell of food hung thick in the air, making my mouth water. I looked around and spotted Eliar seated near the center speaking to someone I didn't recognize, but his eyes flicked to me almost immediately. Zach and Azrin were on patrol today, but they were always back by supper. Everyone was, that was one of Eliar's rules.

I tried to push down my worry and slid into a seat beside Alex and gladly accepted the plate she handed me.

"Are you as hungry as I am?" she asked.

"You have no idea." I said, mouth full of something roasted and heavenly. We were halfway through dinner when Azrin and Zach finally returned. Dust clung to their boots, and their faces were tight with something I couldn't make out. I tried to feel for Azrin's emotions, but he had me shut out, which only added to the anxiety.

Azrin clapped Zach on the shoulder and crossed the clearing toward Eliar, with Zach right behind him. I watched as the three of them stepped off to the side, their voices hushed but appearing urgent.

Apparently, Alex noticed it too. "Something's off." I just nodded slowly in agreement with her, the food suddenly feeling heavy in my stomach.

After the meal, just as I was rising to help clear the dishes, Eliar approached me, his expression was unreadable. "Walk with me?" he asked, tilting his head toward the tree line.

I followed him a few paces from the firelight, the cool air brushing against my skin.

"There's something you need to know," he said once we were out of earshot. "Azrin and Zach didn't see a single Hollow One on patrol tonight."

I just blinked. "Not one?" He shook his head. "Nothing. It was quiet."

Goosebumps lifted along my arms. "What does that mean?"

He took a deep breath and ran his hand through his hair. "We don't know. That's the problem." He folded his arms, voice low. "We are going to send word to other Remnant members and see if they are seeing the same things. If the Hollow Ones have pulled back, it's not them retreating. They're getting ready for something big."

I swallowed and nodded. "So, what do we do?"

"For now, we just stay alert," he said. "Wherever they've gone, whatever they're planning– we'll need to move fast once we know. Rest when you can. Keep training hard. When we know more, we will all need to be ready."

I nodded, fear all but threatening to consume me. "You can count on me."

I tried with everything in my body and soul to mean that and to believe that myself.

Chapter Thirty-Seven

By morning, something felt different. It was in the air, like the quiet before the storm. I strapped my boots on, ignoring the ache in my ribs. My bruises were healed, and my stitches had dissolved, thankfully.

Training had become second nature now. In fact, I'd come to look forward to it. Alex was already waiting for me in the clearing by the church, spinning a wooden staff between her fingers like it was an extension of her body.

"You're late," she said with a crooked grin.

I picked up the other wooden staff off the ground and laughed. "I'm never late, you're just always way too early."

Then we dove right in. Movements sharp and fluid. Sweat built fast despite the cool breeze, and laughter broke through every now and then when one of us stumbled or missed a step. We trained for a while, and as crazy as it was, it was fun to me.

Alex threw a jab. I blocked it, twisting and sending her staff flying to the ground. "Okay," she panted, sitting on the ground. "You're officially annoying." I laughed and stuck out my hand to help her up. "That just means I'm getting better and you're good at what you do."

She grabbed my hand, hauled herself up, and tossed her braid over her shoulder. "You're ready, you know. Even if it doesn't feel like it. And I'll be honest with you, I have more hope now than I have had in a long time, and as scary as it is, it feels good. And it's nice to have a friend like you." She smiled and pulled me in for a hug.

I couldn't answer her. My throat was struggling to keep a lump from forming and my eyes were fighting back the sting of tears. I squeezed her, hoping that it would convey what my words were failing to.

We wrapped up just as the sun passed its peak. Alex clapped me on the back before heading to her tent, while I made my way to the chapel to shower off the sweat and dirt. The soreness after training had gone, which made me swell with pride. I had never been proud of myself before and even if I fail epically in the end, I can honestly say I am proud of what I have been able to accomplish in these last weeks.

It felt good to have a choice, and to choose to fight, when giving up would be so much easier.

By the time I had changed clothes, put on what little makeup I had, and made it to the common area (which is just the new way we call the cafeteria), the others had started gathering together. Plates were clinking and there was chatter everywhere. There was a good feeling in the room. Just being together was the most comforting thing to me right now.

Someone handed me a tray with roasted chicken and potatoes, and it smelled heavenly. I took my usual seat and tried my best not to look at the door every five seconds.

When it finally opened, Azrin stepped through, he looked exhausted. His shoulders were tense, and his jaw was set in a tight line. But the second his eyes found mine, something in him eased.

He crossed the room without a word, like there wasn't a room full of people that he probably needed to address first. "Hey," I said, a smile tugging at the corners of my mouth and every angle of my heart.

"Hey, angel," he murmured, the word quiet and familiar, like it only belonged to me. Zach intercepted him and handed him a tray of food, then Azrin placed himself in the seat beside me like it was the most natural thing in the world, and for a few minutes neither of us said anything.

The hum of voices around us filled the silence. His thigh brushed mine. His presence was like the calm in chaos. I craved it more than I had realized. When I finally looked over at him, his eyes were already on me.

"I hate that this is on your shoulders," he said quietly and urgently, like he needed to say it and get it off his chest before it consumed him. "I hate that every day we get closer to something that could take you away."

I swallowed hard, I was definitely not expecting this. "Azrin-"

He shook his head, eyes slightly fluttering like they were trying to hold back tears. "I know what's at stake. I know you're the only one who can stop what's coming, but that doesn't mean I like it." He paused. "You're strong. You've proved that time and time again. But I still find myself wishing, selfishly, that we could just walk away. That you and I could walk away. That we could disappear and let someone else deal with the darkness."

Emotion swelled in my throat, too big to speak around. I reached out for his hand, and he let me take it. "I want you to have a future," he added. "One that isn't built on sacrifice or pain or even battles that you didn't ask for. One where we're free. And together."

We just sat there for a beat, his hand in mine, the food long forgotten. I stood up without a word and tugged his hand, pulling him behind me. Azrin followed me without question as I led him out the back door of the cafeteria and toward the training fields.

The air was cooler now, dusk settling in, the sky streaked with lavender, pink, and gold. Everyone else was inside. It was just us and the silence of the field where I'd been bruised, bled, and found myself.

I slowed my pace, never letting go of his hand. "This is where I feel strong," I said, turning to face him. "This is where I remember that I've come so far that I barely even remember who I used to be."

Azrin's expression shifted, pain threading through his features. "Piper—"

"Listen, I know you're worried," I cut in, needing to get my point across. "I know you want to protect me, and honestly, that means more to me than I can even explain. But I can't carry your doubts, Azrin. Not right now."

His jaw clenched, but he didn't interrupt. "I need you to believe that I can do this," I said, almost begging. "Not just say it or hope it—but *know* it. Because I do. I've trained until my body screamed. I've prayed until I cried myself to sleep, and somewhere in all that, I started to believe. I believe God brought me here for a reason, and that He's not done writing my story."

A breath hitched in my chest, but I kept going. "Back when I first got here, I didn't feel anything but sadness. I thought that was just...who I was. But now I wonder, after learning and seeing things firsthand, if something wasn't feeding off that. Hollowing me out. Because now—" I looked up at him, my voice thick, "now I feel hope. I feel joy. Azrin, I feel *loved.* And I want to think that I am going to live long enough to feel all of it with you."

His hand lifted slowly, brushing a strand of hair from my cheek. "You think I doubt *you*?" he asked, his voice low and rough. "Angel, I don't doubt you. I'm terrified of a world that doesn't deserve you."

My heart squeezed. "I just—" he broke off, his voice tight. "I've watched the world ruin everything good. I can't let it ruin you. You're the only thing I've ever wanted that didn't come with a price tag written in blood."

I stepped closer, until there was barely space between us. "Then stand with me," I whispered. "Don't stand over me, shielding me. I need people to believe in me like I'm choosing to believe in myself."

Azrin stared at me for a long, charged moment. And then he nodded, just once. "Then with you," he murmured, "I shall stand."

Chapter Thirty- Eight

Weeks had passed in a blur of repetition— wake up, train, eat, train more, shower, eat again, and crash into bed just to do it all over again the next day. The rhythm was exhausting, but familiar. And in some strange way, comforting. Everyone had fallen into their own routines like they'd always lived this way.

But even in the routines, there were moments that still caught me by surprise— moments like this one.

The sun had dipped low, bleeding gold across the field behind the chapel as if it were painting one last picture before night swallowed it whole. The air smelled like dirt and sweat.

Alex and I were finishing drills when she finally threw up her hands. "Alright, enough. You're going to wear my good arm out."

I smirked, lowering my staff. "That's the point. We have to build the other one up."

She rolled her eyes, then smiled. "You're getting faster. Stronger too."

"I feel it," I said, breathing heavy. "Even the soreness doesn't last near as long. Some days I don't even feel it."

Alex clapped me on the shoulder. "I know it may not feel like it, and maybe I shouldn't even say this, but Piper, I think you're as ready as you're ever going to be. I have never seen a human train as hard as you have, or study and learn about the fight ahead."

She gave me a nudge and then she grabbed her towel and headed off toward her tent, leaving me alone in the growing quiet. I lingered for a moment, staring at the spot where our staffs collided over and over, and let myself feel proud. I hadn't realized how much I needed that.

When I made it back to the chapel, I showered, scrubbed off the day, and changed into clean clothes. I even swiped on a little mascara and lip balm, just because I could. And because I wanted to feel like more than just a soldier in training.

The common area was buzzing by the time we got there. The sound of laughter and plates clinking was music to my ears. We were like one big close-knit family. I spotted Alex with Zach, both nursing bruises and giving each other crap about them. Maeryn and Eliar were at the far side of the table talking low, heads bowed like always. I noticed a few new faces had joined us. They were quiet, watchful, and seemingly grateful to be here.

Someone handed me a tray of roasted chicken and potatoes again, and I took my usual seat. I tried not to look at the door every five seconds. Yeah, I tried really hard.

When it finally opened, Azrin stepped through. The noise in the room didn't fade, but my tension did. He looked worn out. Dirt clung to his clothes, streaked across his jaw, and settled in the dark sweep of his hair. His shoulders were tight, wings slightly drooped.

It wasn't lost on me that he came straight here upon returning instead of taking a detour to clean up. Warmth bloomed in my heart.

I focused on my plate, pretending not to notice the way my heartbeat changed when he was in the same room.

When he reached the table, he didn't speak at first. Just plopped into the seat beside me with a quiet exhale that sounded more tired than I knew he would ever admit.

"Hey," I said voice softer than I meant. My heart pulled toward him like it always did. Azrin shifted in the seat beside me with a groan, elbows on the table, hands over his face. Dirt clinging to him like second skin. Seeing him like this tugged on every one of my heart strings.

"Are you okay?" I asked gently. Suddenly hyper-aware that maybe that wasn't the best question because he was obviously not okay.

I could see the corner of his mouth turn up underneath his hand. "I'm better now, Angel."

A tray was set in front by someone passing by, but he didn't move to eat. I watched him, quietly studying the lines around his eyes, the way his shoulders stayed tense even here, even now.

"Did something happen?" I asked.

He shook his head and let out a deep sigh. "Not yet," he said. "But it feels like it's about to. I don't know how to describe it, I just feel like something is building, and I can't figure out what. I have lived a long time, and I have never seen anything like this."

I didn't press for him to explain more. We were all feeling that lately. The atmosphere was thick with a tense anticipation for what the future would bring.

We ate in silence for a few minutes. Or rather, I ate. Azrin pushed his food around his plate, obviously distracted.

I nudged him lightly with my elbow. "Didn't your mother ever tell you not to play with your food?" I instantly regretted it as soon as I said it. Do angels even have parents? I am certainly not doing myself any favors these days. I just want to hide in a hole right now.

He huffed a breath that might've been a laugh, then leaned back, eyes on the ceiling. "Do you ever wish you could just pause time? Maybe push this all back a little further?"

I blinked. "All of the time. But then I quickly remember that I can't, so I train harder, in every aspect."

His gaze dropped to mine again. "You train harder than anyone I have ever known."

That quiet admission wrapped around my heart tight. I didn't know what to say back to that, thanks to my social awkwardness and anxiety. So instead, I stood. "Come with me."

He looked like he might argue, but something in my expression must have changed his mind. He stood and followed me out into the night.

The moonlight was soft, casting the grass in silver-blue shadows. The grass beneath our boots crunched faintly as we walked beyond the tents, past the edge of the chapel's glow.

We stopped beneath the tree line, just far enough for the quiet to surround us. I didn't look at him when I spoke, I instead looked down at the ground. "So, there's something that I have been avoiding since we got here."

Azrin stepped closer, hands in his pockets. "What is it?"

I glanced over my shoulder and then back at the chapel. "My dad's journal, the one that sealed our bond and essentially set your promise to him in stone, I have it but when I arrived here, I put it away and made myself forget about it."

His expression was legitimate concern. I hate that we have to keep our emotions cut off from each other, because now that we have the access, I crave it all the time. "You haven't read it yet?"

I shook my head. "No. I think part of me was afraid of what it would say. Maybe he wrote down that he was going to end his life, and I didn't think I was prepared to find out if he even did or didn't."

Azrin didn't speak, but I felt the weight of his attention. "I took it out tonight," I said. "I don't know, I just felt pulled to it today."

He was quiet for a moment before stepping closer. His voice was calm and soothing. "Do you want to read it together?"

That made something catch in my throat. I nodded slowly. "Yeah. I think I do."

Azrin didn't say anything right away. He just stood there beside me, looking out at the trees like they might have the answers we didn't.

"It's okay if you're not ready. You do whatever you need to do in your own time." A beat of silence passed between us as I let his words sink in.

I glanced down at my hands. "I don't think it matters right now if I'm ready or not. There could be something in here that might help us, and that's more important."

He placed one hand on my elbow ever so gently. "Then I'll be right there with you, if that's what you want." He said simply.

I gave him a smile, hoping it would convey my gratitude in a way I feared my words could not.

We started back toward the chapel in comfortable quiet. The sky had turned a soft velvet color, somewhere between duck and full night. On the walk back I felt that familiar pull toward Azrin, but also a strange new steadiness. I already knew I wasn't alone in this but every day I feel more confident and grateful for my newfound friends, and I'm thankful I have them all by my side.

Inside, the main hall was mostly cleared out. A few people lingered, either laughing at something, cleaning up what little was left from supper, or preparing for their shift for the night watch.

When we reached my room, I hesitated at the door. Azrin placed his hand on the small of my back for soft reassurance. I opened the door, and we stepped inside. I was suddenly feeling very strange for making a big deal about reading a journal. But my dad was and still is a very sensitive subject for me to talk about, let alone read his words and thoughts and see his handwriting.

The journal was tucked in the drawer by my bed, shoved beneath scraps of paper, and knick knacks I have accumulated since my time here. I pulled it out carefully, running my hand over the cover. We sat on the edge of my bed, shoulders just barely touching. I stared down at the journal, heart thudding way too hard in my chest.

I took a deep breath, trying to mentally prepare myself for what I was about to discover. I opened it to the first page.

Piper, if you're reading this, it means I'm gone.

My throat tightened. Azrin reached out and laced his fingers with mine without a word.

I didn't know how to prepare you for the kind of world you'd be left with. I only knew I couldn't protect you forever. So, I wrote this— not to burden you, but to help you remember what's important when everything else feels lost and broken.

Tears slipped down my cheeks, quiet and steady. I kept on reading.

This world is darker than I ever wanted to believe, Piper. But there's still light in it. It lives in people like you. People who choose to have faith, even when all hope feels lost.

I paused, breath hitching.

Azrin's voice came soft. "He knew you'd struggle and find your way back."

"Yeah. Yeah, he did." I replied, voice barely a whisper.

I turned the page. There were more entries, and a few scriptures scribbled around. There were a few questions he seemed to wrestle with. His fears, his prayers, and hopes that he had for me.

We read until the words blurred together. Eventually, I closed the journal and rested it in my lap. "I really thought reading this would be hard and depress me, but somehow, I feel stronger, and I have a strange sense of peace."

Azrin looked at me, something fierce and tender in his eyes. "You are strong, Piper. And now you know that your dad thought about you in every aspect of his life. He didn't make a decision without thinking about you first."

We sat in silence for what felt like a long time. Then, he murmured, "I still hate that this is all on your shoulders."

I turned and looked at him.

"I know you can do it, angel. I do. But sometimes I wish.." He trailed off, jaw clenched. "I just want you to be happy. I want us to be happy. Not constantly fighting for our lives."

My heart pulled toward him like gravity. "I know you do, but I need you to know that I *am* happy. Even with the circumstance, I am the happiest I have been in a long time." I tried to convey my emotions on my face, which was harder to do without the help of the bond. "We may be fighting for our lives, but I see it as I'm fighting for a chance to redeem myself for the past several years, so that when I do die, I have a chance at eternity in paradise. Nothing is more important to me than that, and I'm ashamed I lived for so many years without that mindset.

He squeezed my hand a little tighter. I continued, "I need you to believe with everything you have that I can do this. I need you to know it—even when I'm doubting it myself."

His gaze didn't waver. "I believe you more than I can put into words."

That was all I needed to hear.

Chapter Thirty-Nine

Maybe it was the way Azrin looked at me before he left my room last night, or maybe it was the way he believed in me, even when I struggled to believe in myself, but I felt empowered. After he went back to his room, or tent, (I really wasn't sure where he was sleeping these days, or if he even was sleeping) but I made my way to my cozy cot and collapsed. My muscles ached from the constant training and my heart ached from reading dad's journal. But despite all of that, I had one of the best sleeps that I've had in a very long time.

I woke to sunlight slipping through the gaps in the blinds, warming the air just enough to make it harder to get up. For a few seconds, I stayed still, letting the quiet morning try and convince me that it was a normal day, but I swiftly was reminded that those don't exist for me at the moment.

Voices came from the other side of my door. Familiar sounding ones at that. I sat up slowly, brushing sleep from my eyes. My joints cracked in protest, but I stood and crossed to the door, cracking it open just enough to peek out.

Velicity stood in the hallway, laughing at something Eliar said. Her long braid swung behind her as she hugged him tight, like she hadn't seen him in years. Miriam stood nearby, her arms crossed, already surveying the chapel like she was planning on how she could decorate it. I can't believe they're here.

I stepped into the hallway, and Miriam's gaze found mine instantly. "Good," she said. "You're up."

Velicity turned toward me, her smile widening. "Good morning! Hope you don't mind a surprise visit."

All I could do was blink in disbelief. "What are you doing here?"

Miriam walked closer to me, her voice filled with concern and excitement. "Eliar sent word that things were quiet here and maybe something bigger could be going on. We figured backup might be needed, and we wanted to see you."

I chuckled and nodded. We absolutely needed their help, especially Maeryn. Poor woman stayed cooped up praying and searching for whatever she could to find us an answer or something that could help. However, putting that aside, I was really overjoyed to see them, I missed them more than I would ever admit to them.

With each passing day I felt more and more prepared and confident for what was in store. I truly felt overwhelmed with the amount of support this little chapel, and beyond to the tents, had been given, whether if it's been to one another, or to others outside of this little family.

I felt a strange sense of peace standing there in that moment. I genuinely felt that the weight of the world wasn't anyone to carry alone.

Chapter Forty

Azrin

Seeing Piper smile as genuinely as she is right now is one of the few things that gives me joy these days, aside from Piper entirely. I'd give anything to see her smile like that all the time. Her laugh fills my heart, and whatever room she is in, with joy and hope. It's not that hollow, polite laugh she gives people to be nice, but a real one. It makes my chest ache in a way I can't explain.

I leaned against the window frame on the second story with the church bell, with my arms folded, trying to keep up the façade that I'm keeping an eye out for any potential threats. I hadn't taken my eyes off Piper since I got back from my patrol. After reading her dad's journal with her, I couldn't sleep and had to do something.

She was walking ahead of Miriam and Velicity, talking with her hands, her hair tied in a braid. She looked like she was at peace. And maybe I was crazy, but I don't think I have ever seen anyone look more alive

She was in her element, a far cry from the girl I watched over after her dad passed. She was a force to be reckoned with.

"You're going to burn a hole in her back with that stare," Zach muttered beside me, scaring me a little because I had no clue he had showed up beside me.

"I'm not staring." I said short and a little rougher than I had intended. He just snorted and patted me on the shoulder.

"Riiiight. You're just watching...aggressively? No, protectively. Well shoot, they both look the same on you." I didn't even give him the pleasure of a response, so I just stayed quiet.

"She looks good," he added after a beat, a little more serious now. "She looks happy."

I nodded in agreement, "She deserves to be."

Zach nudged me with his elbow. "You know what else she deserves? A guy who stops lurking in this bell tower and tells her how he feels instead of sulking and brooding."

My head snapped towards him. "I don't sulk. And I don't brood."

He cracked a smile at me. "Mhmmm. Sure."

I rolled my eyes but didn't bother arguing. He wasn't wrong. I hadn't said what I wanted to. Not all of it at least. Some part of me was waiting to see if she changed her mind about me, for this fragile, good thing to slip through my fingers like everything else had.

"She smiles at you by the way," Zach said casually. "When you come back from patrol. She smiles at you every time you walk through the door. And Alex mentioned to me that she constantly looks around for you when you're gone. Worried that you may not make it back through those doors."

My eyes flick to him. But before I could respond, movement caught my eye across the yard. Maeryn's stride was quick, her expression unreadable, and she was heading straight for us. Something about it didn't sit right with me.

I pushed off the wall. "Come on." Still, before I stepped away, I looked back one more time, just in time to see Piper throw her head back and laugh at something Miriam said.

I couldn't help but smile myself. Everything about his woman is so contagious you can't help but feel it too.

Maeryn didn't slow down until she was right in front of us. Her expression was sharp and focused but not panicked. That ruled out an immediate threat, but not something serious.

"We have a situation," she said without preamble. Zach and I exchanged a glance. "What kind of situation?" I asked.

"Not here." She flicked her gaze toward the field, where Piper was still with Velicity and Miriam, unaware.

My stomach instantly tightened. "Is it about her?"

"Sort of." Maeryn hesitated, then motioned for us to follow her. "Come on, Eliar's waiting."

Zach fell in step beside me. "If she says, 'sort of', it usually means yes." We followed her across the yard and into the small side room where Eilar was already pacing. He looked up the moment we entered.

"We intercepted a message," he said without any greeting.

"A message?" I asked. "From whom?"

"That's the thing," Maeryn said, shutting the door behind us. "It wasn't sent to us. It was sent to *her*." Every hair on my neck stood up.

Eliar nodded grimly. "One of our techs flagged it. It slipped through the usual barriers. It was encrypted and laced with Veil energy. Whoever sent it knew exactly how to get around our wards."

I felt my stomach turn. Zach and Alex are the ones who put up the wards, so I know they're strong. It just doesn't make sense.

"What's it say?" Zach asked, his voice unusually quiet.

Eliar looked at me. "It asked Piper to meet alone. No one else. It said she'd know where."

A long silence settled. "She doesn't know yet?" I finally asked.

Maeryn shook her head. "No, we weren't sure whether to tell her. Not until we knew more."

"We don't keep things from her," I snapped, sharper than I meant to. "Not like this."

"I agree," Eliar said calmly. "But we also don't want to panic her before we have a plan."

I could already feel the fire lightning under my skin. If someone was reaching out like this, if they were baiting her, it meant they knew more than we thought, and they have a plan. And if they laid one finger on her...

"We think it's the one controlling the Hollow Ones," Maeryn said. Everything in me stilled.

Zach scoffed angrily. "You think they're calling her out."

Eliar's jaw clenched. "We've never seen anything like this before. Hollow Ones have always been mindless. They've just been shadows feeding on and amplifying sin. But everything that has happened leads us to believe that, yes, someone is pulling the strings. And they want her."

I couldn't move. It suddenly felt hard to even breathe. Maeryn stepped closer to me and picked up my hand and placed it in hers. "She trusts you Azrin," she said quietly. "If this moves forward, she's going to need you beside her."

I nodded once, with no hesitation. "She already has me."

Chapter Forty-One

"I swear, if you two had shown up a month ago, I wouldn't have gotten anything done," I laughed, nudging Velicity with my elbow as we walked past the rows of tents in the backyard of the chapel.

She smirked. "Of course you would've. Miriam would have made it her personal mission to see to it that any training or learning that you needed, would get done." Miriam playfully scoffed and threw in a mock toss of her hair.

I barked out a laugh, one I hadn't heard from myself in too long. Before all of this, I really took these two for granted and I was so determined to be alone and on my own that I made it a point to not get close to them. A decision I felt guilty about, especially now. The weight of the future felt a little less suffocating with them beside me, even if it was only temporary.

We rounded the corner to the chapel, half- talking and half- laughing over a goofy joke Miriam made, when movement caught my eye. Out of the side door stepped Azrin, Zach, Eliar, and Maeryn. They were peeling off from the chapel with a sense of purpose that didn't match the easy pace of the afternoon.

I stopped mid-step. Something about the way Azrin moved made my smile falter. It was too alert and too guarded. Velicity was still talking but her words turned to background noise.

My gaze lingered on them as they made their way to the main doors of the chapel and the doors shut behind them. My stomach dropped. It took everything I had to not run straight after them and demand to know what's going on.

But I trusted all of them and knew that they would fill me in when they could. Or at least I hoped.

We rounded another corner, sunlight warming the stone path beneath our feet. Velicity had started trying to impersonate a few fallen angels during training, the wings and all, and Miriam laughed so hard she started crying. I tried to match their energy and tried to stay present, but my mind kept circling back to Azrin's face, the tension in his jaw, and the way he completely avoided contact with me. Whatever that was, it wasn't normal.

Still, I plastered on a smile and pointed toward what we call the training yard, where Alex stood, her blonde hair tied up in a high knot and a wooden staff spinning in her hand like it weighed nothing. She was barking orders at two poor souls trying to dodge her swings, and neither looked particularly successful.

"There she is," I said. "The fallen angel of bruised ribs and wounded pride."

Alex caught sight of us and twirled the staff behind her back before tucking it under her arm. "Well, if it isn't trouble." She called out with a smile. "New recruits?"

Miriam picked up a staff and started twirling it before dropping it before she made a second twirl. "Hardly," I said. "Alex, meet Velicity and Miriam. They worked at the bookstore with me and unbeknownst to me at the time, are members of the Remnant. When Eliar reached out to other members about the Hollow Ones, they thought it would be a good time to stop by."

Velicity stepped forward, hand on her hip. "You're the one Piper said nearly cracked her rib?" Alex raised a brow and looked at me and the corner of her mouth turned up. "Guilty. Though she's much tougher than she looks."

"She's still standing so, I'd have to agree," Miriam said, smiling.

Alex chuckled and threw her arm over my shoulders. "It's nice to meet the two of you. Piper has become a dear friend to me and I'm grateful that she has you two to keep her on task when I can't. She likes to wander, this one."

Despite the hum of anxiety in my chest, I felt myself relax. Being around people who knew me before all of this reminded me that I was still me underneath the pressures of the veilbreaker. Even with such a difficult task ahead, and an uncertain future, I felt overwhelmed with joy and an incredulous amount of faith that I will get the task done and the good will defeat the evil.

I would make sure of it.

Chapter Forty-Two

Miriam pats me on the back. "Alright, now that I've hugged your neck and made you laugh until you cried, I want to see what you've been learning."

I blinked. "Right now?"

She raised an eyebrow. "Unless you're too chicken."

Velicity let out a very dramatic, and unnecessary, *ooohhh* and Alex, who'd been casually leaning against the worn-out brown fence, pushed off with a grin. "Oh, come on, Piper. You've been working so hard. Show off your accomplishments and be proud of them."

Before I could object, Velicity was tossing me a wooden staff and Alex was putting her hair back up. I reluctantly kicked off my shoes and joined Alex.

We squared up, barefoot, our breath fogging faintly in the cooling afternoon air. The others took seats on the edge of a small wooden platform Eliar had built as a makeshift observation deck. Velicity called out commentary like we were in the middle of some fight club.

It was more like a dance than a match. Alex kept me moving and thinking, reminding me to stay on the balls of my feet. I'd managed to land a clean knock to her shoulder and dodge one of her sweeps. By the time we called it, I was sweaty, bruised, and smiling.

"That was incredible," Velicity yelled over her own clapping. "You've basically turned into a ninja."

I laughed at the comparison. "Thanks, V. I'm just thankful that I don't trip over my own feet and fall on my face anymore."

"You really have come a long way. You've put in the work and had the determination to do whatever it took to get good, and you continue to do so. I'm beyond proud of you, dear friend. It's okay to be proud of yourself too." She patted me on the back, and I gave her a sheepish smile. Even now, I still hate being the center of attention.

The sun dipped lower, washing the yard in gold as we made our way toward the chapel to clean up for dinner. The smell of something warm and garlicky drifted from the kitchen.

Miriam walked beside me, brushing a leaf from her cardigan. "Can I ask you a question?"

I nodded my head, "Well, of course."

She gestured to the building. "This place...it's huge. There are rooms, bathrooms, even those little training alcoves. How in the world did an old church get all of this?"

I smiled, wiping my forehead with my sleeve. "I asked the same question and Azrin said Eliar found it abandoned many years ago. The building was in a very rough state, and the grass was so overgrown it was almost taller than Eliar. He and some of the older members of the Remnant started slowly renovating it. Over time, it became a headquarters, and a sanctuary. Somewhere people could come when they had nowhere else to go."

"Huh." Velicity glanced back at the building with new appreciation. "That's incredible." We split off to freshen up, the hallways echoing softly with voices and footfall.

I had just finished drying my hair when I stepped into the hallway and nearly ran into Zach. "Oh, I'm sorry," I said, taking a step back. "I didn't see you there."

He shrugged playfully. "Oh, sure it's okay. It's not like I'm a huge fallen angel with literal wings or anything." I smirked. "So, I'm the only one that doesn't feed into your ego, and you tease me for it?" He leaned against the wall with a crooked smile. "Well, said ego needs a little fulfillment today." We both laughed, and then his tone softened.

"Hey... I was actually coming to find you." Something in his expression made my stomach tighten. "What's up?"

He glanced over his shoulder, then back at me. "Something's off. The others didn't want to tell you before they had more information, but I just couldn't not tell you. I think whoever is behind the Hollow Ones, is trying to communicate with you. And only you."

My vision threatened to go dark. I blinked, fighting to keep my head steady. His words kept echoing in my head. Is this it? My heart racing and fear rising in every way, I managed to turn and start walking to Azrin's room. I have to know what's going on.

I had a bad feeling when I saw them all together. I should've just followed them. As I got closer to his room, I tried to brace myself for the answers to the questions I would be asking. The pit in my stomach growing larger by the second.

Chapter Forty-Three

The hallway felt longer than usual. Each step echoing louder than it should, and it felt like the chapel itself was holding its breath along with me. I wasn't sure what I expected when I reached Azrin's door, but the knot in my chest tightened with every heartbeat.

I hesitated, knuckles hovering. Before I could make myself knock, the door swung open. Azrin stood there, looking disheveled and exhausted. His eyes landed on me and softened. "Hey angel." The expression on my face must've portrayed my thoughts, because his expression became that of concern. "Let me guess, you heard?"

I nodded. "Zach found me. He told me someone, maybe something, is trying to arrange me to meet with them."

He stepped aside without a word, motioning for me to come in. As I entered, Eliar and Maeryn were already inside. A tension hung over the room so thick it felt like I could choke on it.

Eliar gave me a slight nod, but his expression was unreadable. Maeryn had her arms crossed and her lips pressed together like she was biting back things she wanted to say. Zach entered the room right behind me and leaned against the wall beside the other two, folding his arms.

Azrin shut the door behind me. "She deserves to know."

Maeryn sighed and rubbed her forehead. "We weren't trying to keep secrets. We just wanted to be sure before we dropped this on you."

I stood there looking at each one of them, waiting for someone to explain. Eliar was the first to answer. "It's been too quiet. The Hollow Ones haven't shown themselves in several days, which is highly unusual. They haven't even been seen in the outer towns we've started helping. We thought it was a lull... but then Maeryn started sensing something. A shift, kind of like a gathering of energy."

Azrin picked up where Eliar left off. "It feels like something big is building. We think someone is behind the Hollow Ones, controlling them. We've never seen anything like it. And it appears they're wanting to meet with you for who knows what."

My mouth went dry.

Zach looked up finally. "We don't know exactly what's going on or how long we have, but we do think the time is approaching quickly."

Maeryn met my eyes. "I'm not sure how much longer we can ignore it, Piper. Whatever this is, I get the feeling we are all being watched. And I have no clue what's in store next. Or how long we have to prepare."

I swallowed hard, the weight of their words settling like lead in my chest. "Okay," I said finally, voice low and unsure. "Then we prepare until the very last moment."

Azrin gave me a subtle nod, and one by one, they left the room. Eliar patting me on the shoulder as he walked out, Maeryn squeezing me in a hug, and Zach paused in front of me, obviously conflicted as to what he should do. Hugging me would engage the protective, and honestly aggressive, side of Azrin, but I could tell he wanted to let me know without words that he was there for me. Desperate for this awkward moment to end, I stuck out my fist and we proceeded to bump knuckles. His shoulders sagged with relief, and he walked out of the room.

I stayed frozen in place for a few moments longer, needing just a moment to breathe through the storm inside me. I didn't know what was coming, but I knew I didn't want to face it full of fear.

Azrin stood just by the desk in his room anticipating my next move. I knew he was trying to get a read on my emotions, but we blocked each other out several weeks ago so we wouldn't get distracted in life-or-death situations. I finally moved over to him and wrapped my arms around his waist and rested my cheek on his chest. He wrapped his arms around me and squeezed me gently.

I looked up at him. "I need a little bit by myself, but I'll catch up with you later." I stood on my tiptoes and kissed his cheek. I eased out the door and walked through the chapel, trying to avoid as many people as possible so I didn't get stopped or distracted. Thankfully it seemed everybody was busy doing their parts to make sure everything was ready to grab at a moment's notice.

I slipped out the side door, finding the narrow path that led toward the tree line behind the chapel. It was quiet out there—just birdsong and the faint rustling of the wind through the leaves. I sank down onto the cool stone bench tucked beneath the trees and bowed my head.

God, I don't know what's coming. But You do. I don't want to move forward if I'm running on fear. Help me stay grounded in truth. Help me stay brave. Use me however You need to, even if it scares me.

It wasn't eloquent, but it was honest. And in that moment, it felt like enough. I took a while to sit there by myself, admiring the trees and the landscape. I felt grateful and overwhelmed that we were so lucky to live in such a world that had so much potential if only more people believed or had faith. A part of me felt heavy guilt for the years after my father passing, the way I lived my life with no direction or hope. I knew better but I still lived that way anyway.

By the time I returned, the sun had almost disappeared, save for a tiny peek above the horizon. Supper was almost ready. Laughter floated in from the kitchen, and the warmth of the community was drawing me in like the biggest hug.

I passed Zach in the hallway, who paused long enough to give me a nod of acknowledgment before he disappeared into, what we have started calling, the War Room. It was where we made plans for patrol and kept up to date on what was happening with other Remnant members.

Whatever was coming, I knew we'd face it together. Even if I had the choice of doing this on my own, this family would never let me. My heart filled with an overwhelming sense of gratitude and appreciation. I will never be able to convey to these people just how much I needed them.

Chapter Forty-Four

The sun was beating down on the top of my head, making my black hair hot and seriously making me wish it was a lighter color. Sweat clung to my skin, my lungs burned, and my arms felt like they were made of concrete—but quitting was not an option.

Not with three of the most intense warriors I'd ever met forming a circle around me like wolves waiting for a meal.

"Again," Azrin barked. I adjusted my stance, rolling my shoulders back even though they screamed at me. Across from me, Alex raised her staff, twirling it once with a smirk. "Don't blink, Pipes."

To my left, Zach tossed me a short blade. "Work on your reflexes. And don't be afraid to use your elbows, in a moment of desperation, they can be your best weapon."

I caught the blade, barely, and pivoted just in time to deflect Alex's first swing. She didn't go easy, and I knew better than to expect her to.

This wasn't regular training. This was high stakes, and I quickly realized that they all have been holding back way more than I could've guessed. They didn't wait for turns. Alex pressed forward, her staff aiming low, Zach darted behind me to cut off my retreat. Azrin hung back like a shadow, watching every move I made. Calculating.

I knew they were preparing me. The Hollow Ones wouldn't wait politely for me to finish with one before another joined in. They'd swarm and overwhelm.

So, despite their current training tactics, I knew it was for preparation and not cruelty. I took a blow to the ribs, staggered, and dropped to one knee. I shot back up with a growl, swinging the blade and landing a solid tap against Zach's shoulder.

He grinned ear to ear. "There she is."

Alex winked. "If we can get you to quit thinking and distracting yourself, you'll be in good shape." Azrin still hadn't moved. His eyes locked on mine from across the training field. "Again."

Eventually, Alex called for a break. Zach tossed his blade aside and flopped dramatically in the grass. "I'm not saying you beat me," he huffed, "but I am definitely going to need an ice pack later."

I smirked, doubled over and bracing my hands on my knees. My lungs were craving for air, and I was pretty sure my legs had turned to jelly. "You're just saying that because I hit harder than you expected. That, and you're out of shape."

He pointed a finger at me without looking up. "Exactly. And I'm not out of shape. You're just getting better at keeping up with me."

Alex handed me a water bottle, her cheeks flushed, and her braid half undone. "That was solid, Piper. You're reacting faster and moving smarter. Keep that up and you'll be able to take two down at once."

"Only two?" I teased, chugging the water.

She grinned. "Let's not get cocky." Azrin hadn't said a word. He stood just beyond the edge of the training ring, arms folded, expression unreadable. When I made my way toward him, he didn't speak at first, but he did hand me a towel. His eyes searched mine. "You're stronger, faster, and way more patient and disciplined in your movements." I gave him a big smile, something about getting praised from him made my heart flutter.

Before I could respond, Alex's voice called out. "Uh hey guys, the clock is ticking. If we don't eat soon, Zach may start eating us."

That earned a muffled "I heard that!" from Zach, who was still laying on the ground but had rolled over onto his stomach.

Azrin glanced at me once more. "Go clean up. I'll see you at supper." He gave me a wink, and I tuned toward the chapel grinning at how pathetic my friends were.

My arms and legs were beyond sore, but the uncertainty of the future started to creep its way in. If I fail, what would it mean for fallen angels? For my friends? For the world? The amount of pressure is unbelievable, but I'm not alone, and its not my burden to carry alone. We are a team, and we will either prevail together, or fall together. Preferably prevail but together is best.

I washed up quickly, the sting of warm water on my sore muscles somehow grounding. As I ran a towel through my hair, I caught my reflection in the small mirror above the sink. There were still dark circles under my eyes, but I didn't look sick or hopeless anymore. I looked, and felt sharper, stronger, and more confident. I felt good.

Dinner was simple—roasted vegetables, rolls, and something Velicity had declared 'a culinary masterpiece' but it tasted, and looked, like beef stew. Still, it was hot and filling, and absolutely delicious.

Alex had taken up her usual spot at the far end of the table, boots propped up, arguing with Zach over the better way to win a sword fight. I genuinely cannot believe this is my life, if someone would've told me 5 months ago that I would be sitting here with fallen angels, cut off from the rest of the world, learning to sword fight, preparing to essentially save the world, and fight demons, I would have never in my wildest dreams believed it to be true.

Maeryn had reappeared from wherever she vanishes to during the day and gave me a small, reassuring nod and smile.

Azrin sat across from me, a quiet presence as always. He didn't say much, but his gaze flicked to me every now and then like he was trying to get a read on my feelings. "I'm glad we trained today," I said, nudging a piece of bread across my plate. "I needed it. I feel way more confident now." I hated it, but I was starting to feel like Azrin was pulling away from me. He was quieter around me; he was just giving off a vibe that formed a pit in my stomach.

His bright green eyes met mine. "Angel, the demons have no idea who they're up against. You are a force to be reckoned with. You kept up with two, annoying, but very skilled fallen angels. Who, mind you, have been around for an incredibly long time." I couldn't help but smile ear to ear, his pride was absolutely radiating through his voice and through his eyes. I felt silly for the way I was feeling 20 seconds ago.

His confidence in me had a way of sinking past all my walls and spreading warmth and happiness. As the meal wound down, conversation shifted toward the mundane—how the supplies were holding, which nearby towns needed another check-in, and how the chapel roof had a leak in the sanctuary that needed to be fixed before the next rain.

A quiet tension still hummed under the surface. I don't know if I was more sensitive to the supernatural now, or if I was just hyperaware of the Veil because of my duty, but I could feel it thinning. Eliar announced that tomorrow we'd be splitting into groups again to reach out to the Remnant members in the outer towns. No one ever reached out after Eliar sent the first round of messages, but Velicity and Miriam had received it, so we were unsure what had happened. The Hollow Ones also hadn't shown themselves in almost two weeks, and while that should've brought relief, it only made us more uneasy.

Azrin caught my eyes again, and something in his expression said he was feeling it too. A shift in the air. The kind you couldn't explain but knew better than to ignore.

We were running out of time

Chapter Forty-Five

Sleep did not come easy. So much was weighing on my mind and heart that I couldn't make myself fall asleep. The morning light felt different. It wasn't golden or soft like usual. It was pale, almost cautious, as if the sun itself was hesitant to rise. And maybe I was just looking too much into that as an overthinker, but it surely fit the mood.

I stood by the window in the small room I'd claimed, staring out at the tents and trees beyond the chapel walls. People were already in motion, packing supplies, taking inventory of our weapons, reloading water bottles.

Today is the day we all split up. Alex was going with Eliar. Zach was pairing with Maeryn. Azrin would be staying behind, continuing to train the few of the members that could see the demons due to their strong faith and commitment. And I was meant to be resting, recharging, and clearing my mind so I can be at my best.

There was something special about the way the swords gleamed in the light, lying across the table near the chapel's entrance. Not because of the steel, but because of what they represented. Every blade had been blessed, each edge dipped in holy water and prayed over. They were our only weapons. And we didn't have enough of them.

My eyes drifted toward the center of the yard, where the others were gathered with Eliar who was inspecting gear. I wasn't sure what I was expecting but I was so shocked when I saw the chest plates and pieces made specifically for our thighs, upper arms, and any major body parts.

I rested my forehead against the window for a moment, breathing in deep. This was happening. A lump in my throat rose and I didn't feel ready, not even close. This whole thing is surreal to me. It's hard for me to remember a time before all of this. I was just a regular person doing regular person things, but I had no idea the Hollow Ones existed, and maybe my father did tell me, and I just ignored him.

It is crazy to now know this side of things and to have the knowledge that I was feeding Hollow Ones during my years long pity party. Ever since I met Azrin and came here, I feel so much different. I can think clearly and just breathe without it feeling like a ton of weight is sitting on my chest.

The fact that this was all happening around me my whole life and I just couldn't see it, is enough to blow my mind.

I am blessed to be on this side and to help the people of the world who are being fed on by the demons and who can't see because their faith isn't where it could be or simply because they just haven't had a conversation to lead them to the opportunity to grow. No matter the reason, I want to make sure that there is a future where people can choose light over darkness.

I reached up and wiped at my eyes, not even realizing tears had formed. Not from fear this time, but from conviction. If everything I'd gone through was what it took to bring me to this moment, to this purpose, I'd do it all over again. A quiet knock sounded at the door.

"Angel?" It was Azrin's voice, but it was gentler than usual.

"Yeah," I called back, clearing my throat and dragging my sleeve across my face. "Come in."

He stepped inside slowly, his eyes scanning mine like he always did. "We're about to go over last-minute travel details before the groups head out. Eliar thought you should sit in, even if you're not going."

I nodded. I did appreciate them keeping me in the loop no matter what. "Okay. I'll be there in a second."

Azrin lingered, his gaze immediately showing concern. "Are you okay, angel?"

No. Yes. I don't know. "I'm as good as I can be. I am just feeling the pressure a little bit heavier today, as I'm sure everyone is." I said honestly.

He gave a slow nod, like he respected and understood my answer. He gave me a quick kiss on the top of my head and quietly closed the door behind him. I let out a breath and looked around the small room that had somehow become my safe place. I took a moment to enjoy the quiet and soak up the peace.

Then I put on my boots, pulled my jacket tighter around me, and followed him out the door. Azrin had already disappeared when I entered the hallway. It was quiet, but the low hum of activity echoed faintly through the walls. I made my way toward the kitchen, figuring I could grab an apple or something quick before the meeting. I wasn't exactly hungry but having something in my stomach might help keep my nerves in check.

As I stepped into the kitchen, I spotted a woman struggling to balance a stack of tin serving trays and a woven basket filled with rolls. She was older, maybe in her fifties, with deep brown skin, graying curls sticking out from under a scarf, and an easy strength in her posture despite the wobbling load.

"Need a hand?" I asked, stepping forward. She looked at the tower, startled at first, then gave me a grateful smile.

"I'd love one, actually. These trays seemingly have a mind of their own."

I grabbed the top half of the stack and steadied the basket while she adjusted her grip. Together, we made quick work of the awkward balancing act, setting everything down on the long counter at the far end of the room.

"Thank you," she said, brushing her hands off on her apron. "I swear, it's like every meal is my own personal battle lately." She chuckled.

I smiled at that. "You're doing the real work though. You manage to make three meals a day, feed at least, I'm honestly not even sure how many people are here, but I know it's a ton. You keep this kitchen running all hours of the day. I think it's safe to say, on behalf of everyone, it is very much appreciated."

She gave me a warm look, and a soft smile. "I may be managing the battles in this kitchen, but I don't do it alone, thankfully. You're fighting the ultimate battle. I've seen you out there training, you couldn't pay me to be a Hollow One at the other end of your blade."

I felt my cheeks redden. "I'm doing the best I can. Thank you for saying that, though."

"I'm Janice," she said, extending a hand.

I shook her hand. "I'm Piper."

She nodded like she already knew. "I can't imagine how you must be feeling, especially these days, but I can tell you that the people in this camp, and the other members beyond, will help you in every way they can. Just like we all know you'd do for us, and anyone really. Your commitment and faith continue to build hope and stronger faith in each of us. Even those of us who can't see what you see yet."

Her saying that meant the world to me. Hearing that makes me want to try that much harder and do that much better. I felt a lump begin forming in my throat.

"Well," I said softly, "believing sometimes matters more than seeing."

Her smile widened and her eyes twinkled. "Amen to that."

A voice called out from down the hall, reminding me of the meeting I was supposed to be attending. I pointed to an apple in the fruit basket in the center of the counter and gave her a questioning look. She smiled and nodded.

"Thanks for the help," I said. She may not have helped me physically, but I needed this conversation. She helped my nerves and strengthened my confidence.

She waved me off. "You're the one who helped me, sweetheart."

And with that, I stepped back into the hallway, heart a little lighter. Strengths came in many forms. Some people wielded swords, and others wielded gentleness and kindness. And I was starting to realize, we needed both.

I followed the hum of quiet voices down the hallway, biting into the apple as I walked. The sweetness helped settle the nerves still flitting around in my chest like restless moths. The room wasn't anything fancy, it was just a cleared-out chapel classroom with mismatched chairs and a table pushed to the side to make space. A few maps were pinned to the wall, and someone had scrawled notes across the whiteboard on black marker. I slipped in and took a seat near the back just as Eliar stood up front, arms crossed, gaze sharp.

Alex gave me a small wave from across the room. Zach gave me a small nod. Azrin didn't look at me, but I could feel the awareness between us like a tether.

Eliar cleared his throat. "Thanks for being here. I know not everyone will be leaving, but this affects all of us and I feel it's best for everyone to be on the same page and aware." He gestured toward the maps. "The outer towns have been quiet, a little too quiet for our liking."

Alex leaned forward. "Do we know if the Hollow Ones are regrouping? Relocating?"

Eliar shook his head. "We are not sure. That's what we are hoping to find out. Alex and I will head east to Harren's Bend. Maeryn and Zach will go north to the forest routes we haven't checked in weeks. We'll avoid confrontation unless it's unavoidable. These are scouting missions, not attacks."

Zach raised a brow. "You're sending me and Mae Mae into the trees, and you think it's not going to be confrontational?" Zach's attempt to lighten the mood earned a few light chuckles but the tension in the air was like a live wire. It was hot and intense.

Eliar nodded toward Azrin next. "Azrin's staying behind. We still need to continue to train. If anything happens here, this will be the first line of defense."

Azrin's voice was low but firm. "We'll be ready." Everyone then turned toward me. I felt it even before I looked up.

"And Piper," Eliar said gently, "you're not on the front lines today. You've been training hard and pushing harder. We need your mind sharp and your spirit rested. So, rest, study, relax as best as you can."

I nodded slowly. "I understand."

Maeryn added softly, "We have established we don't know what's coming, we just know something is. And we all need to prepare—physically, spiritually, and emotionally."

The room stilled for a long moment.

Then Eliar gave a tight nod. "Gear up. We leave in thirty."

With that, chairs scraped, boots and shoes scuffed, and quiet murmurs rose as everyone moved with purpose.

I stayed seated a moment longer, staring at the map. At the black X marks scattered like bruises across towns.

The war wasn't waiting anymore. It was on its way.

Chapter Forty-Six

Standing in the front of the chapel tonight felt strange. We put everything in the back or slightly off to the side. Watching them load up their things into the vehicles made my stomach feel funny. But we needed to know.

We said our goodbyes and one by one, they disappeared beyond the treeline. I stood just outside, hands tucked under my arms as the wind bit at my skin. I should've gone back, but something made me stay. Maybe it was guilt, or maybe it was the sucky feeling that nothing after today would be the same.

Azrin stood beside me, quiet as ever. After a few more moments of freezing and standing in silence, I turned to go inside. There wasn't much to do, but somehow everything felt urgent. The remaining people were already in the courtyard, training or continuing to work on supplies. I joined them, lending a hand where I could. Whether it was refilling water bottles, helping stack firewood, or helping clean tents. I was trying, really trying, to stay in the moment. To not let the what ifs cloud the little peace I still had.

But my mind kept drifting. "You're going to chew a hole in your lip." Azrin's voice said behind me. I turned, caught off guard by the teasing tone. He was leaning against the chapel's doorway, arms crossed, watching me with that unreadable expression.

"Sorry. It's just that I hate feeling helpless, and I hate waiting."

He nodded. "I hate it too. Waiting is where doubt and fear grow best. But hold on to the fact that each of them is skilled, and they can hold their own."

I gave a small smile and nodded my head.

I walked toward him, brushing my hands off on my pants. "So, what do we do now?"

He turned and looked at the group of people working and training hard, and he took a deep breath. "Now, we continue doing what we've been doing. We prepare. Spirit, mind, and body. Whatever's coming—we meet it head on."

By lunchtime, we'd gotten a lot accomplished. We all decided that since we were unsure of what information we'd be told when the others got back, we'd clean up the whole place so we could focus on the task at hand.

We'd swept and mopped every square inch of the chapel. The tents had been tidied, and laundry had been washed and hung in the sun. We cleaned every blade that wasn't taken and even cleaned debris from around the chapel grounds. It felt good to do. It was something we could control and that was much needed in this situation.

During the cleanup, I realized how much I was missing my friends. Only four people were gone, yet it felt like so much more. I knew they would return. But the air felt thinner without them. The energy was definitely quieter without Zach. It almost felt like the heartbeat of the place had slowed.

I have appreciated getting to know some faces that have been here for a while that I hadn't gotten to know yet. There were several fallen angels here as well and although they do tend to be a bit more stand-offish, it was fun watching these huge men learn how to sweep and mop. I still hadn't realized how much space my friends took up until they weren't in it, and it made me sad. I won't take it for granted when we are all back together.

After lunch, everyone pitched in for a faster clean up and I think we were all just needing to feel helpful and were finding joy in doing acts of service today. The dishes were finished, and the counters were wiped clean. It was very comforting having everyone work together like a big family at a holiday dinner.

Azrin called for everyone to meet near the training circle. His voice wasn't sharp, but it carried authority, the kind that didn't need to shout to be heard. I brushed my hands off on my pants and followed the others, still chewing the last bite of a biscuit one of the nice ladies handed me after lunch.

By the time I got outside, Azrin was already dividing people into pairs. A few fallen angels were showing some of the other Remnant members some defensive blocks. Some of the others stretching or joining together in prayer. The air buzzed with preparation, but underneath it, I still felt that strange stillness again.

Azrin spotted me and nodded. "Angel, you're with me."

I blinked. "Wait, what about me taking it easy?"

He smirked and winked at me. "I know you and I know that if I don't let you train now, you'll just be out there after everyone is asleep, when you should be sleeping too."

I didn't argue. Partially because he was absolutely right and partially because I was itching to be active. After this is all over, I am definitely going to get a gym membership. He handed me a practice blade. "You'll start with me, then rotate. You'll fight Zach's cousin, Rion, next. He's got speed. Then Hadria— she's unpredictable. You need to be able to hold your own against different types of opponents. And opponents that likely won't feel bad if they hurt you."

I nodded, gripping the handle on the blade. Azrin stepped into position, and the sparring began. He didn't go easy on me, not that I expected him to. He swung with precision and power, testing my reaction time, my focus, my ability to perform under pressure without cracking. I blocked the first few strikes, barely, my arms shaking from the force of it. Each time steel met steel, the vibration echoed through my bones.

"Faster," he said, not unkindly, but firm. "You won't have time to think when they come at you. You may not even have a second to react."

I adjusted my stance and took a deep breath, pushing everything else out of my mind, from the ache in my legs to the weight of knowing how high the stakes were. Azrin came at me again, and this time I anticipated him. Not perfectly, but better. I ducked low and aimed for his side, but he deflected and twisted behind me before I could blink.

"Good," he said. "Again."

We moved like that for what felt like hours. My body soaked with sweat, muscles screaming, and lungs burning. But I didn't stop.

Eventually, he called a break. "Rion, you're up."

Zach's cousin stepped forward, twirling his blade like it was an extension of his arm. "Zach and I may be cousins, but make no mistake, you're completely overmatched," he said with a crooked grin.

He was fast. Faster than I could track at first. I had to rely on instinct, not sight, and that alone changed how I moved. He was graceful and sharp. "Don't think so hard, just move, Piper," he said after I misjudged a parry and nearly lost my grip. "You've got the heart and determination for this, just make your mind and body follow suit."

When he finally tagged out, I was gasping for air. My arms felt like they were hanging on by threads, and I was fairly certain I'd have bruises come morning.

And then came Hadria. I didn't know what to expect, but it wasn't the whirlwind I just faced. She didn't announce her presence, and she didn't banter like Rion. She just attacked. There was no warning and no rhythm. It was like fighting a storm. Every move was intense and unpredictable. She spun the blade like a dancer might twirl a ribbon—beautiful and dangerous.

I gritted my teeth and stayed on my feet, refusing to falter, even as she knocked the blade from my hand once. And then again.

Azrin didn't interfere. He watched silently from the edge, arms crossed, and I knew why. I needed this. I needed to be able to look death in the face and still find a way to get back up.

By the time it ended, I was on the ground, chest heaving, and blood pounding in my ears. Hadria offered me a hand up. "You're not bad," she said. "But if I were a Hollow One, you'd be gone."

I accepted the hand and stood. "Good thing you're not one." I managed to breathe out. She smirked and walked to the small table that held water bottles by the fence.

Azin walked over and clapped a hand on my shoulder. "You didn't quit, angel. I know it seemed tough and believe me I wanted to help you, more than you can even begin to know, but we could get separated and I needed to know that you can handle yourself until I can get back to you."

I didn't have the breath to respond. But beneath the soreness and fatigue, I felt something burning brighter. Resolve.

Chapter Forty-Seven

I stripped off my sweat-drenched clothes and stepped under the weak stream of the shower, wincing as the water hit sore muscles and bruised skin. Every part of me ached. My arms, my back, even my fingers from gripping the blade too tightly. Maybe going that hard today wasn't the best idea but, I really should've been doing that this entire time.

Still, I was proud. Exhausted...but proud. I leaned my head against the tiled wall and let the water run over me, trying to slow my thoughts. I wanted to stay in here forever, but the scent of food wafted in, and I was starving.

After throwing on a hoodie and brushing through my tangled hair, I strolled into the hallway and into the main dining space. Plates clinked, quiet laughter floated through the room, and for a moment, it felt almost normal.

I moved slower than usual, every step a reminder of today's training, but I still helped carry a few bowls and wipe a table off. As I eased into a seat, I couldn't help noticing how different it all felt. Four people missing, and yet the void was immense.

No sooner did I finish that thought the when door leading outside swung open. All conversation ceased. Alex stepped in first, Eliar followed closely behind. Alex looked like she hadn't slept. Her hair was tied back in a loose braid, and a jagged tear in her sleeve revealed dried blood. Eliar's expression was unreadable, per usual, but there was a sharpness in his eyes I hadn't seen before.

He scanned the room, locked eyes with Azrin across the table, and said urgently and seriously. "We need to talk. Now." The entire room froze. The weight of Eliar's words was enough to snap everyone's attention into place.

Azrin was already pushing back from the table, his chair scraping the floor. Eliar held out his hand and motioned for me to come as well. "Piper, come with us please."

Azrin and I trailed behind them into the room up the hallway. I clicked the door shut behind us.

Alex leaned against the table with her arms folded. Her face was pale, but her voice was steady. "There is no good news. It's exactly as we've been suspecting. We found a perimeter with runes etched into the buildings like some kind of containment or warding circle. But it didn't appear to keep them out, it looked more like it was keeping them in."

A chill slid down my spine. "What does that mean? Why are they being contained?"

Eliar looked at me, then glanced at Azrin. "We don't know. We couldn't get close. Every time we tried to get close, something just felt... wrong. We are thinking it's like their headquarters. It's hard to explain, but I think we have been right this whole time. I genuinely believe they have a master."

Azrins jaw flexed. "You're saying that someone, something maybe, is controlling them?" Eliar nodded his head. "It explains everything that's been happening. And just from what we saw and felt, there just isn't another explanation for it. I've never seen anything like it or heard of anything like this happening."

My heart is racing, and my hands are clammy. "So, what do we do?" Eliar looked at each of us in turn. "We keep as we have been. Most importantly we dig into every scrap of old prophecy and scripture Maeryn's ever seen. We pray and we armor up in every way possible."

Alex gave me a look I couldn't quite distinguish. Part admiration and part sorrow is what it looked like to me. "Piper. You can no longer go anywhere alone. Not anymore.

You're the key to stopping this and they know that. If they kill you, we have no chance."

A growl sounded from my left. I looked over and Azrin's face filled me with terror. Not because he looked afraid, but because he looked furious. His jaw was clenched so tightly it looked painful, and his hands were fists at his sides. There was something dangerous and raw in the way his chest rose and fell, like he was struggling to keep himself contained.

"They will not touch her." He managed to get out. It was only when his gaze slid to mine that I realized what this was. This wasn't fear of the Hollow Ones, this was fear of *losing me.*

"Azrin," I said softly. His eyes locked on mine. The room melted away, and for a moment we were the only two people in it. "I won't be reckless," I promised, trying to steady my voice. "You trained me yourself, trust that you did a good job and I'm as prepared as I will ever be. You don't have to worry."

His throat worked as he swallowed, but he didn't say a word. Instead, he reached out, his fingers brushing mine before curling into a tighter fist and dropping to his side again. Then he turned and walked away, shadows trailing like smoke behind him.

After Azrin left there really wasn't much talking after that. Alex was desperate to shower and Eliar wanted to document everything he saw while it was fresh on his mind, so I retreated back to my room and let the silence cradle me. My mind was loud with everything Eliar had said.

I moved on autopilot, brushing out my hair again, washing my face, and brushing my teeth. I folded my jacket and set it on the chair, then sank down onto the cot and pulled the blanket over me. I stared at the ceiling for a long time.

The chapel was quiet now, save for the occasional creak of the roof or soft rustle of the wind outside my window. Eventually, my eyes grew heavy, and sleep overtook before I even realized it.

* * *

I didn't know what woke me, the cold sweat on my skin, the pounding of my heart, or the unmistakable feeling that something was irrevocably wrong.

I sat up slowly, every nerve in my body on edge. And then I heard it. A sound outside the window. Soft at first, then it got louder. Like claws scraping against stone. My breath caught in my throat as I crossed the room and pulled the curtain back.

My heart dropped. They were here. Hundreds of them. Shadows slithering through the trees. Eyes glowing like embers.

We were surrounded.

Chapter Forty-Eight

Azrin

I shot upright in bed, heart pounding like I'd been yanked from the depths of a nightmare. Her fear was real—so raw and overwhelming it stole the air from my lungs.

We'd practiced keeping the bond closed for weeks, but her end was wide open right now, and my angel was beyond terrified. I threw off the blanket, barely registering the blade I grabbed as I shoved my feet into my boots. I'd felt her afraid before, several times, but this was the kind of fear that paralyzed, that sunk its teeth in and didn't let go.

And she was alone.

I bolted from my room, the hallway already humming with something dark. Something was definitely off. I focused my hearing, and I heard it. A sound I'd heard too many times before to ever mistake again. The Hollow Ones were here. My blood ran cold. But Piper—*my angel*—was still in her room.

I ran as fast as my legs would carry me. I barely rounded the corner before the chaos swallowed me. Boots thundered down the hall. Voices shouted over one another. Fear clung to the air like thick smoke. And beneath it all, I could hear the clash of metal and screams. My mind was being pulled in a million different ways, but I needed to get to Piper first.

"Get to the tents!" someone barked, and I turned just in time to avoid colliding with two older Remnant members, swords in hands and rushing for the doors.

"Azrin!" a younger man I didn't know well, Samuel is his name, I think, grabbed my arm, his eyes wide with panic. "They're everywhere, man. We're surrounded."

"I know," I snapped. "Get outside. Anyone who can fight, fight. And anyone who can't, help tend to the wounded. Keep the inner halls secure."

"But what about—"

"*Now!*"

He flinched and ran. More bodies clogged the hallway. The air was hot and suffocating. I shoved my way forward, not caring who I jostled.

Piper's fear still pulsed through me like a second heartbeat. I could feel her panic, grasping for control, but she wasn't able to get a foothold. She was spiraling.

Hold on, angel. I thought. *Just hold on. I'm coming.*

The next hallway was worse. Two demons had slipped inside and were being held back by three of our own. Their snarling faces turned toward me, but I didn't stop. One lunged, and I ducked beneath its clawed swing, driving my blade through its gut in one smooth, practiced motion. It disintegrated into smoke and ash as I kept moving.

I started shouting her name the moment I hit her hallway. "Piper!" There was no response. I screamed louder. "Piper!" My heart slammed against my ribs. I reached her door and kicked it open so hard the hinges broke.

But there she was. Frozen and pale. Her eyes locked on the window where the demons crept like shadows across the lawn. "Azrin—"

"I know, baby." I was already at her side, already pulling her back from the glass. "First things first, I need you to take a deep breath. You need to shut the door to me, your fear is all I can feel and think about, and I need to think clearly right now, okay?" I placed a hand on either side of her face, forcing her to focus on me.

She nodded swiftly, closed her eyes, took a deep breath, and I felt her emotions leave and close completely off. I hated doing that because it always felt cold and empty after, but this was imperative.

She opened her eyes. But before she could say anything I cut her off. "Great. You stay behind me. Okay?" She nodded. Her eyes held something other than terror. Determination.

"Alright, come on, angel. We've got a fight to win." And in that moment, with the weight of uncertainty pressing down on us, I leaned in and kissed her.

I pulled back just long enough to press my forehead to hers, her breath still mingling with mine. The next second, I was sprinting out the door, trusting her to stay behind me.

The hallway was still chaos. The sound of steel clashing and cries from the outer camp pushed through the stone walls. My pulse quickened, and I couldn't get out there fast enough. "Eliar!" I shouted over the mess of voices, grabbing one of the younger Remnant by the arm. "Where is he?"

He nodded his head toward the door at the end of the hall. "He's already outside. He said the east side is already overrun!"

I shoved through more bodies, issuing orders as I went. "If anyone is combat-trained, get out there and help!" A few nodded and peeled off toward the doors. Others looked to me for more direction, but I didn't have time to hand-hold.

I pushed forward, dodging shoulders and stumbling feet as more of the Remnant poured into the halls. The sounds outside were getting louder.

Piper was right behind me, her footsteps light and steady. Even if our emotions were closed off, I could still feel her, thanks to our tether.

I reached the entrance just as the doors were thrown open. Night air rushed in, thick with ash and smoke. The east side of the yard was overrun just like I was told. Tents had been torn down, flames were flickering from almost everywhere, I couldn't make out much more than that. I caught sight of a demon lunging for one of ours, and then a flash of steel as someone brought it down.

I spotted Eliar barking orders, and I made a beeline for him. "Where do you need us?" I asked, already surveying the battlefield.

"They came through the wards," Eliar said, his voice a mixture of panic, confusion, and anger. "That should've never been possible."

My chest clenched. "It's not. Unless someone let them in." His eyes flicked to mine, and I saw it hit him too. "Zach and Maeryn..."

I nodded. "They haven't come back yet," I finished for him. "And only the Remnant or the fallen we agreed upon can bypass the wards."

Piper's eyes widened, the same realization dawning on her face. "No way. I refuse to believe it."

I shook my head, my jaw clenched tight. "We don't know anything. Right now, all we know is that two people are missing, and only one of us could have let them in."

From somewhere behind us, someone screamed. A tent collapsed and the fire was spreading. Piper stepped closer to me, and I placed a hand on her back without thinking, anchoring her to me.

"We need to hold the yard," Eliar snapped. "Alex is on the west line. You guys take the east, drive them back or we're finished."

I nodded once. "We're on it." Piper didn't wait for me to pull her along. She moved with me, eyes sharp and spirit rising like the flames. We joined the line on the far side. My blade handle was already slick with sweat from the heat of the flames.

Out of the corner of my eye, I caught movement in the tree line. I recognized the figure almost immediately.

Zach.

Chapter Forty-Nine

I blinked, making sure I wasn't imagining it. But I knew I wasn't. He was so real, and he was looking right at us. I lowered my blade an inch, stunned.

"Zach?" I breathed. I wasn't sure if I said it aloud or if I thought it.

Azrin moved first, stepping in front of me protectively, his body taut with the kind of tension that always meant danger. I couldn't help but feel confused. Where was Maeryn? And why weren't his hands stained with blood and ash like everyone else's?

Then I saw it. The flicker of the flames illuminated his face just enough for me to see the smirk on his face. Azrin growled and shoved me back, raising his blade. "Stay behind me."

"No," I said, my heart splitting. "We need to know what he's—" But then it all made sense. The wards, the breach, everything. Eliar was right. Only someone from inside the Remnant could've opened the way. The world around me tilted. It's been him all along. He pretended to be my friend.

Tears threatened to fall down my face. Everything inside me cracked open, like glass shattering, under the weight of this heart-breaking betrayal.

He vanished into the trees a second later, gone before I could even scream after him. Azrin caught me by the arm. "We need to get to Eliar. Right now."

"But Maeryn—" He started pulling me toward the last place we saw Eliar. "Piper, we have to get to Eliar, Mae is not with Zach, someone needs to find her."

My stomach dropped. How had we not seen it? How did *I* not see it? Azrin's hand was still gripping mine as we ran. The fires roared louder, and so did the fear in my chest. We didn't have time for anything but fighting. But as I looked over my shoulder back into the trees, I was sure of two things. The first being Zach had declared war. Secondly, I was going to end it.

We found Eliar again near the chapel steps. He was barking more orders, and drenched in sweat, blood, and ash. When he saw us, he didn't ask questions, he made a circle motion around the whole camp. "They're pushing through everywhere. We're severely outnumbered."

Azrin opened his mouth to speak, but I cut in. "It is Zach." Eliar's face went still. Confusion, sadness, and fury all took turns showing in a matter of seconds. "We saw him," I said. "He's here. He's the one who let them in and who is controlling them."

Azrin stepped closer to Eliar. "Maeryn's not with him. I don't know what he did, but she wouldn't have helped him with this. He's working alone from what little I saw."

Eliar's jaw tensed. "Then we've got more problems than just Hollow Ones." I nodded, already following Eliar's train of thought. "The wards. He knows how to break them. And they keep pouring in."

"He won't stop," Azrin added. "Not until we stop him."

A beat passed. Just one. That was all Eliar gave it before he turned back to the battlefield. "Then we end it." He looked at me, but not as the girl who purposefully ran from her faith, but as the Veilbreaker I'd become.

"This is it, Piper. Are you ready?"

I looked at the chaos happening around me. "No," I said honestly. "But I'm doing it anyways." Azrin gave a single nod, then turned and sprinted toward the east side of the line, again. I followed without hesitation, weaving between tents and bodies, my boots sliding on the ash-slick grass. The sound of clashing steel and the Hollow Ones screeching had almost become a terrifying rhythm, but something else tugged at my focus. It felt like static in my chest, a magnetic pull tugging me forward.

"Azrin," I called as I caught up. "I think he's close. I'm pretty sure I can feel it."

Now that I'm thinking about it, I would always get this feeling around Zach, but I didn't know it was him nor what the feeling was. Now, I know. My Veilbreaker senses felt it the entire time and I had no idea.

He didn't question me. He let me take the lead and I veered toward the trees at the camp's edge, my blade already drawn. My heart thundered. And then we saw him.

Zach stood in the clearing, calm and composed. There were several demons hovering behind him like dogs waiting for a command.

"I was wondering when you'd come," he said, low and deep. It didn't sound like the Zach I knew at all.

Azrin stepped in front of me intuitively, his stance tense. "We trusted you." He snarled. Zach smiled, but it didn't reach his eyes. "I did what I had to do. You don't understand. None of you do."

"Then help me understand," I pleaded, stepping around Azrin.

Zach's eyes locked on mine. The chaos behind me is unbearable but if I can reason with Zach, I can end this.

He chuckled eerily. "You think you're different? That this time the Veilbreaker will win? I've seen this story before,

Piper. Again, and again. A chosen one to defeat the darkness and restore hope, but then... nothing. Just even more darkness. Every time we push back, it returns stronger."

My throat tightened. "So what? You gave up?"

"No," he snapped. "I decided to *end it*. If darkness is inevitable, then I'd rather be the one holding the reins. At least then, I can shape what's left."

I stared at him. "You've become the very thing we're fighting against."

"No," he said quietly. "I've just stopped pretending that the light always wins." He took a deep breath, then continued. "I thought I had the last Veilbreaker on my side," he went on, his voice hardening. "But he never could make a choice. He saw both sides, but in the end, not choosing was his downfall."

My stomach twisted. "The boy," I breathed.

Zach's eyes flicked to mine, and for a second, something like regret passed over his face. "He wanted to believe in the light. He wanted to trust it would be enough. But the world crushed that belief right out of him. I had already fallen by that point, so I had nothing to lose by trying to nudge him a little."

Behind me, Azrin's breath caught like he'd been punched in the gut. His voice came out low and furious. "He was mine to protect."

"And you failed," Zach said, blunt and unapologetic. "You all did."

Azrin stepped forward, keeping his blade drawn. "For years I blamed myself for missing something. I fell because I couldn't face home, not knowing where I went wrong. I fell because of you."

An icy silence fell between us.

"You don't want to save the world, Zach. You want to rule over its ruin." My voice was soft and sad despite my attempt to try and keep my composure.

"Well, Pipes, that's better than burning with it." My heart thundered. Not just from fear, but from pure fury. The sheer audacity of this guy.

Azrin stepped beside me. "Then you leave us no choice."

Zach laughed. "You're not going to kill me." His eyes settled back on me. "And she doesn't have it in her to kill me."

My fingers curled at my side, fists trembling with the anger building inside me. He was right, I didn't want to kill him. But I could stop him. A thought jumped in my head, and I think it could work but it'll be risky. "Luckily, I don't have to kill you to end this."

Zach tilted his head, brow furrowing. 'What do you think you're going to do, Pipes? Talk me down? Tell me I'm better than this and we can talk it out?"

"No," my voice was calm now. Unshakeable. "But you're not the only one with a connection to what's beyond the Veil."

His smile faltered.

Shadows whipped toward me like claws, curling into the form of a Hollow One. Then two, then five. I stepped back, pulse racing. Zach kept his cold eyes on me, not making any effort to move, but he didn't have to, they moved for him.

"Piper," Azrin warned. I could feel the hilt of the sword in my hand getting heavier by the second.

The first demon lunged. Before I had time to register the movement, Azrin intercepted it midair, blade slicing through smoke, the crack of bone reverberating through the trees. The creature shrieked, dissipating behind him. Another slammed into his side, causing him to stagger.

Zach took a step closer, "You think you can win? You think you're better than those who have tried before you? I know you feel the power, Piper. I know you can see the thread. You can feel the pull. Join me and you can have it too."

More Hollow Ones surged forward. Azrin's wings flared wide, knocking two back in a violent gust. There were just too many. They circled us, pressing in. Panic filled my lungs, stealing my breath with every passing second.

Cold, excruciating pain shot through my arm. I let out a hiss. Anger, fear, and adrenaline pumping through my entire body. The pull in my chest flared into pain, causing me to drop to my knees.

Zach took a few steps closer, shaking his head. "Such a shame, Pipes. I really thought we could be in this together."

The air shifted and suddenly, I couldn't breathe. It felt like the air was being stolen straight out of my lungs.

Azrin roared and lunged at him. Their collision shook the entire clearing. Power detonated outward– ash exploded everywhere, tress bending under the force. The Hollow Ones screamed in response, like a battle cry, cheering on their Master, all while never taking their attention off me.

Air filled my lungs, and the world started coming back into view, just in time for me to see Azrin in mid combat, pushing Zach back a step. Then another. Zach locked eyes with me and the smile he gave made my entire body run ice cold.

Darkness surged through and around him like a wave. It hit Azrin full force, pushing him back a few feet and dropping to one knee.

"Azrin!" I screamed with everything I had.

He risked a glance at me. Determination was etched all over his face. He gave me the smallest nod.

In that moment, something inside me locked into place. Trust. I am not in this alone, and I never was. The static in my chest sharpened– no longer a chaotic mess, but peaceful and still.

The tether had revealed itself. It was ugly, tangled around Zach's soul liked barbed wire.

I stood up and made my move, Hollow Ones snarling and making awful choking sounds as they tried to get a hole of me. The closer to Zach I got, the angrier and louder the Hollow Ones seemed to get.

I was almost to Zach when mind-altering pain seared through my lower back. I spun around to an army of demons behind me. I raised my blade and tried to defend myself as best I could while still trying to get to Zach.

Defeat seemed to be imminent. I could feel hope slowly being lost and I was getting desperate. I knew Azrin was getting tired and I had no idea what was happening at the chapel.

Tears were falling from my eyes and sobs were escaping my throat. I made one final swing of my blade and made a turn and ran for my life toward Zach, Hollow Ones right on my feet.

"Piper, no!" Azrin's voice rang out. I didn't stop. I needed to win this. I clumsily grabbed Zach's shoulder and reached for the tether. My hands burned as I grabbed hold of it. And with one movement, I jerked and it shattered.

Screams split the air, not just from Zach, but from every single Hollow One themselves. One by one, they turned to ash, disintegrating. Zach fell to his knees, gripping his chest. "What did you do?"

"I set you free," I said, trying to catch my breath.

"But there's one more thing." Azrin stepped beside me, gaze dark and lethal. Behind us, Eliar and Alex emerged from the trees, joined by a few of the other fallen.

One of the fallen, whose name I was unsure of, moved forward. His eyes, pale like the moonlight, glowed with something ancient.

"This ends now," the angel said. He knelt and pressed two fingers to Zach's forehead. Zach thrashed, but there was no use. A mark shimmered briefly, almost like the wards I've seen, then his body went still. The darkness vanished from his eyes and everything that set him apart of the mundane people, vanished in a blink.

He looked up at me. "Why didn't you just kill me?"

I crouched in front of him. "Because that's not justice. This is. You get to live out the rest of your days as the very thing you were trying to rid the world of. Human."

Azrin moved next to me. "No more manipulation. This is what you deserve."

Zach looked at the ground, then slowly, he looked up at me. "So, what now?"

I didn't answer right away. The battlefield was quiet now. Smoke lingered in the air, curling around us like the last remnants of a storm that had finally passed. I looked at Zach. Really looked at him. Not the power hungry fallen who had nearly destroyed everything, but the man underneath that. "You don't get to ask that. You chose this."

He held my stare, but I caught the flicker of regret in his eyes. It was too late for that now.

Zach didn't resist when Alex and Eliar grabbed each of his arms, hauling him upright. His eyes remained on the ground, shoulders sagging beneath the sudden weight of mortality.

"We'll take him to the council," Eliar said. "We will let them decide what's to be done." They led Zach back through the trees.

Azrin stepped beside me again, hand brushing mine. 'We should head back too," he suggested. "The others will definitely need help."

I turned toward the smoking horizon where our home waited. "Let's go."

Together, we walked back to our family, unsure of what to expect when we got there.

Chapter Fifty

The night had been long and endless. We spent it dousing fires and tending wounds, with trembling hands and aching muscles. Some injuries were serious, like burns, broken bones and deep cuts, but by a miracle, none had been fatal. When Azrin and I made it back to the chapel, Maeryn almost knocked me down with a hug and explained that the Hollow Ones had her guarded and when they disappeared, she came straight here. Miriam and Velicity both embraced me in hugs and praises too.

The chapel stood tall and proud today, but the tents, the outside supplies, and the fragile sense of stability we'd built, was gone. I slipped away while the others continued to work, needing space, needing a moment that belonged to no one but God and myself. My boots crunched over scattered debris and charred ground as I walked into the sanctuary.

It hadn't changed. The stained-glass windows still glowed with soft color and the altar stood steady and unbroken. I made it two steps from the altar before my knees gave out. I hit the floor hard, bracing myself with my hands on the cold floor. It wasn't pain or exhaustion that brought me down, it was gratitude. Overwhelming, heart-jerking, breath-stealing gratitude.

Tears blurred my vision as I lowered my head. My eyes caught something glistening in the soft sunlight. *Ashes.* The veil had torn, a war had raged, and yet, God held the ultimate line.

Behind me, footsteps creaked. Azrin stood in the doorway, shoulders squared, and eyes locked on mine. "Angel, are you okay?"

I nodded slowly, wiping my face. "Yeah," I answered. "I think I finally am."

He crossed the room and knelt beside me, following my gaze. His hand slid into mine without a word. Together, we stared at what remained. Not in fear or grief, but in reverence.

Ashes beneath the altar. The final remnants of a fight we'd survived.

www.ingramcontent.com/pod-product-compliance
Lightning Source LLC
LaVergne TN
LVHW100520110826
845146LV00002B/713
9798995474203